Queenstown ~~Search & Rescue~~

Time for a rescue of their own?

Best friends—and search and rescue volunteers!—
Mallory, Kayla and Maisie battle the elements and
save lives on a daily basis. Now there is a
new challenge on the cards for them: love!
Are they ready to open their hearts to three
unexpected love interests?

Find out in…

Captivated by Her Runaway Doc

A Single Dad to Rescue Her

From Best Friends to I Do?

Available now!

Dear Reader,

This is the third and final book in my Queenstown Search & Rescue series. It has been fun to write and I hope you've enjoyed getting to know the characters throughout the series.

We've seen Zac Lowe and Maisie Rogers in the other stories and now it's time for them to find the romance that has been missing in their lives. But it's not easy when they've been close friends since they were teenagers when Zac became a part of Maisie's family. It's a big step for Zac, and he's afraid if it all goes wrong, then he'll lose the people most important to him, including Maisie.

For Maisie, who is recovering from a broken marriage, trust is a huge issue and she knows she can trust Zac, but can she give him her heart? She's tough, but is she tough enough to survive a second broken heart? But when she can't not love Zac, all she has to do is persuade him they're on the right track for love.

I hope you enjoy following their journey to love.

All the best,

Sue MacKay

FROM BEST FRIENDS TO I DO?

SUE MacKAY

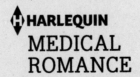

HARLEQUIN

MEDICAL
ROMANCE

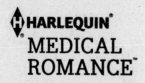

HARLEQUIN®
MEDICAL
ROMANCE™

Recycling programs for this product may not exist in your area.

ISBN-13: 978-1-335-40892-1

From Best Friends to I Do?

This edition published by arrangement with Harlequin Books S.A.

For questions and comments about the quality of this book, please contact us at CustomerService@Harlequin.com.

Harlequin Enterprises ULC
22 Adelaide St. West, 40th Floor
Toronto, Ontario M5H 4E3, Canada
www.Harlequin.com

Printed in U.S.A.

This book is for my family. My man,
Lindsay MacKay. And Hannah MacKay and
her man, Phil Grigg, and Austin and Taylor Grigg.
You are all so special and I am lucky to have you.

Sue MacKay lives with her husband in New Zealand's beautiful Marlborough Sounds, with the water on her doorstep and the birds and the trees at her back door. It is the perfect setting to indulge her passions of entertaining friends by cooking them sumptuous meals, drinking fabulous wine, going for hill walks or kayaking around the bay—and, of course, writing stories.

Books by Sue MacKay

Harlequin Medical Romance

Queenstown Search & Rescue

Captivated by Her Runaway Doc
A Single Dad to Rescue Her

London Hospital Midwives

A Fling to Steal Her Heart

SOS Docs

Redeeming Her Brooding Surgeon

Take a Chance on the Single Dad
The Nurse's Twin Surprise
Reclaiming Her Army Doc Husband
The Nurse's Secret
The GP's Secret Baby Wish

Visit the Author Profile page
at Harlequin.com for more titles.

PROLOGUE

MAISIE ROGERS SNIFFED, then blew her nose and wiped her eyes with her sleeve. Today her sister would've turned eleven. Instead she was stuck at ten—for ever. She'd never grow up and wear high heels or go on a date or become a ballet dancer like she'd wanted to be. All because of an ice cream.

No, Maisie, blame the driver of the car that hit her on the pedestrian crossing she was dancing across.

Scrubbing her face with her knuckles, she felt a change in the air, and stilled.

'Bad day, eh?' Zac Lowe sat on the bench beside her outside the classroom block at Queenstown High School.

'It sucks. It's the worst time since Cassey died.' Her heart began thumping weirdly as she looked at Zac. All out of rhythm.

'It is.' Zac rubbed his shoulder against hers

like he was sharing something more than a bad day with her.

His touch was different to what she was used to. Usually he acted like a second brother. This prickly, exciting sensation spreading out from her shoulder made her lean closer for more. 'Thanks for being with me.'

'It's okay,' he muttered before shuffling sideways, putting space between them as he glanced around the grassed area in front where others were standing talking or girls strutting in front of guys.

Maisie leaned nearer again, not wanting to lose the feeling he caused. She also needed his support and company. Today was truly awful. And now confusing.

Zac and her brother, Liam, became best mates a year ago when they'd started playing in the same rugby team. Now he was always there for her, and, like Liam, overprotective since her sister's death. It was bad enough having her brother and father watching over her friendships and what she might be up to without adding Zac to the equation. 'Everyone says it'll get easier with time. I don't believe them.'

He straightened away from her again. 'I guess no one really knows what to say.'

As usual, he was right. It didn't lessen her pain any. 'I wouldn't mind a hug.'

To be held in your arms and feel what it's like to press against your chest.

Her cheeks heated.

Zac looked around, fixed his gaze on someone at the far end of the block.

Liam stood yarning with some friends, looking over their way, a frown marring his forehead. What was that about? Since he'd brought Zac home after rugby practise one afternoon Zac had quickly integrated into her family, her parents giving him support where he required it at school and with his sporting activities and in other areas when needed. Zac muttered, 'We're at school. Everyone's out here.' The gap between them had widened further.

'You can't hug me?' Her hands clenched and her head spun as she fought the need to throw her arms around him, to show him what she felt. He was cool. He didn't have a girlfriend. She didn't have a boyfriend. He was seventeen to her fifteen. What was the problem? More likely grief about her sister was screwing with her common sense, and it had nothing to do with Zac. Maybe he was just Johnny-on-the-spot.

The hell he was.

He was fun and strong and gorgeous, and she wanted to get close to him. She'd love to know him as a hot guy who might look at her similarly, and not as her brother's mate. To feel special as a girl, to have him want to spend time with her. To be the first guy to kiss her.

'No, Maisie.' He unfolded his long body from the bench and stepped away from her, leaving her lonely and cold.

'Why not?' Her feelings and needs hadn't been written all over her face, had they? Too bad, because they were real. Zac was amazing.

'Think about it. Everyone'd be talking about us. That's not happening. Some girls might get the wrong idea and upset you.'

'Stop trying to protect me from everything. I'm sick of you all doing that. I'm quite capable of looking out for myself.' Except she *was* hurting and it was getting her down. But she needed cheering up, not cosseting. She needed Zac holding her against him, sharing himself with her, rubbing his hands down her back, touching her as she'd never been touched before. Except he'd just shown her he wasn't interested in her in that way. She'd have to hide her feelings and get over him as soon as possible.

* * *

Zac stared at Maisie, his heart in his throat. He wanted nothing more than to hug her, hold her close, feel her warm body pressed into his. He'd wanted that for a long time now. If only it was so straightforward. But. He drew a breath. It was a huge but.

He couldn't touch her, not even in a friendly way. One day her father had caught him watching Maisie with the hunger in his belly no doubt apparent in his eyes, and said, 'I'm sure there are plenty of suitable girls at high school for you to take a fancy to. Stay away from Maisie.'

She was too young, and too vulnerable since her sister's death. Being the quiet, un-assertive one of the family, it was everyone else's role to make sure she was safe.

Given that this family had all but adopted him, given him the love and constancy he'd never had with his own parents, he'd known he had to shut down his feelings for Maisie. Touch her and he'd lose what was so, so important to him. Lose his go-to place and the people who'd enabled him to face the world with confidence when his parents didn't, and never had. They'd never been there for him, too busy with their seven-day super-ette and so tied up in themselves as though they couldn't accept they even had a second son. Their first had died before he was born. Which was why nowadays, if he had a problem, he went straight to one of Maisie's parents for advice and comfort.

It was so damned hard not to reach for Maisie and hold her as a young woman and not his sort-of-sister. Those big brown eyes with cheeky golden flecks were so hard to ignore, even when filled with sorrow. Especially then. But to tuck her against him now would only lead to more problems for them both.

So he turned away, saying over his shoulder, 'See you tonight.' There was going to be a special dinner at the Rogers house in memory of Cassey, and naturally he was expected to be there. This was the first time he'd ever wished he had an excuse not to be. The raw pain in Maisie's eyes had grown when he'd pulled away from her, making him feel guilty, and unworthy. He needed to toughen up, be the protective friend he was meant to be. Ask one of the girls in his class to go to the football team's end of season party next weekend if he wanted a bit of passion. That might quieten the hormones for a bit.

Sighing as he strode across to Liam and their mates, he knew there was more than hormones involved in how he felt about Maisie, but her father was right. This wasn't the time or place, if there ever would be.

CHAPTER ONE

MAISIE HANDED THE bridal bouquet back to her best friend, Mallory, who had just exchanged wedding rings with Josue, and hugged her. 'I'm so happy for you both. It's about time one of us was married.' Quickly turning away, she discreetly wiped her eyes, careful not to be seen so her friends couldn't give her a hard time about being sentimental. But hey, who wouldn't be when Mallory had tied the knot with a gorgeous Frenchman only minutes ago?

A sharp elbow prod from the second bridesmaid, her other close friend. 'Mallory looks beyond happy, doesn't she?' Kayla finger-wiped beneath her eyes.

Okay, so tears were allowed. 'About time she found her soul mate,' Maisie agreed. Mallory had done a better job of picking a great man than she had. *Her* marriage had been over within twenty-four months, and

now she was a whole lot wiser about men
and how they could lie to break her heart.
When she'd met Paul, she'd naively jumped
in without a thought, accepting his love and
charm, believing she'd moved on from her
teenage crush on Zac. Not once did she con-
sider Paul might hurt her. But now wasn't the
time to be thinking about that particular pain
in the backside. Today she was happy for her
friend, and also just plain glad to be back in
Queenstown amongst family and friends for
the wedding. She'd be back permanently in
a few weeks.

Her gaze drifted sideways to scope out
the guests. Zac stood with a group from the
Search and Rescue crew, looking breathtak-
ing in a dark blue suit and crisp white shirt.
Stunning. Hot. He was not a man for her to be
noticing that way—certainly not to be thinking he was even a *little* bit hot. She'd deliberately not thought any such thing about him
since that day sixteen years back when she'd
been so sad about Cassey and reached out to
him because she'd yearned to get close, only
to be rejected. At the time she'd wondered if
he might want to be more than a friend, but
he'd quickly dispelled that idea by walking
away and joining her brother. She believed
she could trust him to always have her back,

but for anything else? When she'd learned the hard way not to trust any man with her heart? No, not even Zac. She'd read him wrong once, wasn't giving it a second crack, even if she was older and, hopefully, wiser.

She looked back to the bride, and sucked in air to settle her nerves. Zac was definitely hot, but nothing would come of that.

Mallory was laughing and saying something about how Maisie and Kayla should have another shot at getting hitched because it felt wonderful. Kayla replied it was too soon for her, and winked at Maisie. 'Guess that means you're next.'

No way. She so wasn't ready, and doubted if she would be this side of another decade.

Mallory suddenly threw her bouquet straight at Kayla, who caught it and tried to hand it back. Relieved it wasn't her who'd been targeted, Maisie laughed and hugged Kayla. 'They'll look nice in a vase on your table, if nothing else.'

'I could force them on you,' Kayla muttered.

'No, thanks. I'm happy being a free agent.' That was a loose term considering she wasn't on the dating scene at all. Again Maisie's gaze went to the men standing to one side of the aisle, and her skin tightened. Zac was looking at her with a hunger she'd not seen before. Desire for her? Surely not. In a blink the longing disappeared from his expression, replaced with the cheeky twinkle she'd grown up knowing. He must've realised she was watching him. Relief edged into her head, dousing the bizarre sense that something was out of alignment here. It wasn't like they'd ever been anything but friends. At fifteen she'd learned friendship didn't suddenly change to deep love and sex. She shivered. Zac and sex?

Not so hard to imagine. He was sexy. She'd always thought so. Occasionally, after leaving Paul, she'd wondered what might've transpired if she and Zac had got together when they were younger. Back then she'd been afraid to follow up on the feelings of tenderness and adoration, her lack of confidence stonewalling her. When he'd walked away that day, she'd accepted far too easily that he wasn't interested. The ensuing mixed emotions over Zac and her sister's death had caused endless sleepless nights and moods that drove everyone crazy for months.

Kayla said, 'Here comes the champagne.' She accepted two glasses from the young waiter's tray and handed one to Maisie.

Time to refocus on the happy couple in

front of her and why she was here. 'We've all come a long way from three skinny little runts on the first day of school.'

Laughing, Kayla tapped their glasses together. 'Hopefully this will keep you from coming out with more daft things like that.'

And keep me from glancing across to Zac every few minutes trying to understand that look I saw in his eyes.

'You think?'

Except she didn't have to glance any more. Zac stood in front of her with a wicked grin as he raised a glass of champagne to her. 'You're looking very swish.' That *sounded* like the man she knew.

'I can scrub up with the best of them.' She sipped her champagne before looking directly at him, trying not to flinch as her skin tightened again.

His expression was clear of anything out of the ordinary. 'It's been a while since you last came home for a visit.'

'Over two years ago.' Before her world imploded. 'You know I'm moving home permanently for the job in the new paediatric department next month, right?'

'Your memory failing?' His grin was that silly brotherly one he'd given her most of their lives.

Disappointing for some reason, she thought, before getting back on track. 'I've already told you.' But she wasn't sure he'd remembered, because nothing seemed normal at the moment.

'Often.' His grin dipped as he sipped his wine, his eyes meeting hers over the rim of the glass, that cobalt shade sharper than she could recall noticing before. 'You're really ready to pack up and come home now?'

'The packing's all done.' Along with her family, he'd tried to persuade her to return to Queenstown before Paul's trial but she'd refused, insistent that she stay and face everyone who'd thought she'd been a part of the scam where her charming husband had convinced pensioners to invest their hard-earned life savings in his schemes. Schemes that were illegal and put money into his personal accounts, not investment plans. Some people, including a couple of friends, believed she had to have known and was as guilty as Paul. Others accepted she mightn't have, but she'd lived a comfortable life on the benefits so owed something to the victims. Few saw her to be as much a victim as they'd been. 'It's time to let the past go, to move on with my choices for the future.'

She was getting there by herself, without her brother and Zac butting in and taking over as they liked to do, and that made her feel good about herself. There was still a way to go, especially when it came to trusting people. She'd given her all to Paul, believed in love, believed he loved her back. Except she'd been wrong. He'd used her as part of his charm package to get older folk on side with his investment schemes that she'd had no idea about.

Those intense eyes were still locked on her. 'You know what you want?'

Her mouth dried a little. Because Zac *was* looking at her differently. As if he was seeing her as a woman and not the sister of his mate. Not his surrogate sister. But he couldn't be. She had to be making it up, seeing things that weren't there. Was she that desperate to find love? Not likely when she wouldn't trust a man with her heart again. Another sip of champagne moistened her dry tongue. 'I've got the job I'd been hoping for back in the town where my closest friends live, and Mum and Dad. It's all I've hoped for over the last year.' The plan was what got her through the worst days.

'It's something to start with and further along than you've been in a while.'

'I also intend buying a small apartment when I can afford it, but that's about it for now.'

Eventually a man I can love and trust would be great. A family too.

'You've never mentioned that before.'

'I don't tell you everything I hope to achieve.' With all the phone calls they'd shared over the last year, they'd covered a lot of ground but not everything. Certainly not another relationship or one that might involve children.

'Fair enough.' Did he have to look disappointed?

'I think so.' This discussion felt stilted, unlike the easygoing, almost intimate conversations they were used to having on the phone. Then again, she'd been stunned to see the way he was looking at her, and didn't quite know where she stood with him.

Zac took a gulp of his champagne, smiled crookedly. 'I'll talk to you about possibly joining Search and Rescue once you're settled in. We can always do with more medical personnel.'

The tension creeping in backed off. That smile always softened her heart. 'You're on.' She gave one back. 'I'm excited about coming home.' She'd been quick to get away from her over-protective family—and Zac—when she left school, and yet it was the first place she wanted to be when her world went belly-up. This was her comfort place where she knew so many people and fit right in.

During the last twelve months they'd spent more time on the phone discussing how Zac was coping after a shooting incident where he'd been injured when a gunman went crazy and killed one of the police team Zac had been a part of, and less about her and Paul. She hadn't wanted to share all the details with either Zac or her family, preferring to sort it out herself. So far she had, which made her proud, and stronger than the shy girl who'd left town twelve years ago at the end of school to train as a nurse.

When she met Paul, he'd charmed her, wooed her with an ease that should've been a warning. But she'd fallen in love instead, been too naïve and ready to forget how she'd once felt about Zac. Her family and friends never took to him, which only made her more determined to prove she was right and could look out for herself. She'd been too vulnerable, too ready to believe she needed Paul by her side, and thought love was supposed to be for ever, through thick and thin, good and bad. Yet she'd fallen out of love with him fast. How could she not when the exciting trips he took her on, the surprise dinners, the jewellery she'd find under her pillow as a surprise, had been paid for with other trusting souls' money?

'Photo time.' Kayla tapped her arm. 'You two will have to carry on catching up later.'

Maisie glanced to Zac. 'No problem. We'll have plenty of time after the dinner and speeches.' It would be fun to sit down with him and get back into the relaxed swing of things they usually shared. As long as she didn't put too much out there, like these mixed feelings of tension and longing filling her.

'Save me a dance later.' Zac grinned, this time looking comfortable.

'Sure will.' Dancing would be something new for them. Even more difficult were the tingles going up and down her spine, and the flare of heat in her cheeks.

They didn't just have one dance. The music that was played after the dinner was slow and sensual, and the air laden with laughter and happiness. Maisie couldn't have walked away from Zac if she'd tried.

He held her waist and led her around the floor so sure-footed that she relaxed into his arms and went with him, cosy and happy. His body was lean and muscular, his shoulders wide and strong. His face was endearing and his mouth soft yet firm. This was the man she'd known for ever, and she'd never seen him like this. Never felt hot and vibrant like this. Too much? Yes. Pull back? Impossible. Or was it that she didn't want to? Zac would never deliberately hurt her, but that didn't mean she wasn't vulnerable to him. More so, because she trusted him completely.

His hand was splayed over her lower back and she could feel each individual fingertip pressing into her. Protecting her from other dancers when they got too close.

'You know the moves,' he said beside her ear.

'Just following your lead.' It wasn't hard when her body was glued to his.

The music stopped.

'Want to continue?' he asked quietly against her ear.

'You bet.' She grinned. This was amazing. So different from anything she'd ever done with Zac. But then no one climbed trees or played cards at a wedding. 'I'm having a ball.' She really was, and waking up to a new side to Zac. A warmth that she'd not felt with him before, a tingle in her toes and heat on her skin.

Zac'd never do something so despicable as

to rob people and abuse their trust. Nor would he con her.

Is this why I'm seeing Zac differently to the friend he's been? I can trust him, believe in him and not have everything thrown back in my face? Is this why I'm suddenly looking at him in a way I haven't since I was fifteen and buried my feelings? I'd be safe with him.

Or was she making another big mistake even considering Zac as more than a friend? Looking for a relationship she wasn't ready for because she knew he'd always have her back? Someone she believed she could trust? She'd thought she had that once before and look where it got her.

Rein it in, Maisie. Don't rush into these feelings and lose a special friend because you've been an idiot.

Straightening just a little, she held herself slightly away from that tempting body, and kept dancing.

'Zac, line three,' the police station receptionist called. 'It's Jamie.'

His Search and Rescue offsider calling during work could only mean one thing. Picking up the phone, Zac answered. 'We're on?' He was head of S and R, but sometimes the calls went direct to the fire station where Jamie worked.

'Yep. A thirty-two-year-old man's fallen off a climbing face in the Remarkables. We need to go in, retrieve him and get him to a point the chopper can safely lift him out. You available?'

'You bet.' It was after four and the day had gone on for ever, every hour dragging by as though two as he'd trawled though files on a cold case murder that new info had come in about. Better than the night hours spent thinking about Maisie and holding her supple body in his arms as they danced at the wedding. It had been everything he'd imagined for a long time—and more. She was real: warm, soft and so sexy when her body moved against him in time to the music. What a turn-on, and something he'd fought to keep in check. Since he was a teen he'd had feelings for Maisie, but suddenly they'd burst wide open. It was exciting, wonderful. Yet caution ruled. What did Maisie think about him? She'd moulded into him as they danced, which upped his hopes she might be changing how she felt. And reminded him of those long, sometimes intense, phone conversations they'd shared when he'd talked about the shooting and she talked a little about Paul's betrayal.

Since the wedding he'd had coffee with her once after helping move her few pieces of furniture left over from her marriage into her brother's apartment, which happened to be in the same complex he lived in. When he'd asked why she had so few items she'd snapped, 'I didn't want anything he bought.' He couldn't argue with that, and had struggled not to take her into his arms then and there and tell her he'd always be there for her. But he hadn't, because he was afraid he might show her his real feelings, and get knocked back. His parents had always ignored his attempts to show he loved them. They'd lost their firstborn at ten months old, and when he'd arrived unplanned for, they must have shut down on him for fear of going through the anguish they'd suffered over his brother's death. No wonder he'd grabbed with both hands the love and support offered by Maisie's family. He only hoped he could give as much love as he received, not only to his surrogate family but to the woman he longed to settle down with. Maisie.

'Hello?' Jamie cut into his thoughts.

Some fresh air and a bush rescue would be a perfect distraction to this love winding through him.

'We flying in?' It was part of his contract

with the police department that he could drop everything for S and R.

'Sure are. I'll pick you up in five. Got one more call to make.' Click. Jamie was gone.

That one more call must've been to Maisie because she was waiting on the footpath outside the hospital when they drove up. 'The man's companion describes severe injuries,' Jamie said as he braked. 'Who better than a nurse in the circumstances?'

'Can't think of anyone,' Zac grunted through the happiness spilling within him as he watched Maisie get into the back of the vehicle. So much for a distraction. Spending time with her only cranked up the need he'd come to expect every time he saw her these days. The feelings he'd had for her at seventeen had intensified over the years, added to by her being so damned attractive and sexy at Mallory's wedding. Then the dancing, holding her close, feeling her warm body under his palms, breathing the floral scent that was Maisie—of course he couldn't sleep the night through any more.

'Afternoon, Zac,' she said now.

'Hi. You were working late.'

'The ward was busy so I stayed on, keeping an eye on a six-year-old girl recovering from a ruptured appendix.'

'You've settled into the job quickly.' She'd

been back in town three weeks and already seemed busy with work, S and R and her friends and family. Not so much with him. His choice. For now anyway. There was some thinking to be done about this need to get to know her in new ways. Once he'd have ignored it and got on with life but now he found he just couldn't put his longing aside. Deep down he had been hoping she'd return home and he'd be here for her. Maisie *was* special, more than a friend. 'What to do?' was the big question. Her family were a huge part of his life and getting too close to Maisie could jeopardise his relationships with everyone if it all went south. Her parents had taught him to be loved and to love back, but was he good enough to love their daughter? He could only work hard to prove he was.

'I love paediatrics more than any other specialty. All those kids needing my help and being able to make them smile or laugh always makes my day.'

Despite his misgivings, the pure joy in her voice made him smile. Quiet Maisie had toughened up a lot since Paul Harris came to light as a lowlife. Not that *he* or Maisie's family had ever liked him. Though there could've been a streak of jealousy on his part, having never quite managed to stop caring for her.

Probably the reason his two attempts at relationships had failed.

Paul had been too full of himself and a right old charmer when it came to getting what he wanted. Maisie had fallen hard for him, and there'd been nothing anyone could say to change her mind. It had been a case of wait and be ready to step in after everything turned to dust. Except when it did, she'd refused help, shocking him and making him sit up and take even more notice of her. Maisie was still the same girl he'd fallen for, only with strength and determination added to the mix. Qualities he was happy to see. Add beauty and sexiness and there was no resisting her. She was gorgeous and those attributes had tightened his groin when watching her walk down the aisle in front of Mallory. Her laughter thickened his blood. And her smiles softened his heart.

How did Maisie see him? Still the guy who'd become a part of her family, to be teased, annoyed and loved like her brother? Whenever they'd talked about the shooting that saw him in hospital and Benji dead, she'd been caring and compassionate, intense sometimes, not quite Maisie as he'd known her. The phone calls had made him feel they were in a bubble, sharing their problems, having a laugh, even shedding a few tears once when talking about lost dreams. But he still had no idea if she might reciprocate his feelings even a little, though the way she'd danced so close to him at the wedding had him wondering if there was a spark there. Forget sparks, his body had reacted like an inferno.

This waiting and wondering wasn't doing him any good at all, but he knew this was something to take slowly, or there could be repercussions. If she wasn't ready for a new relationship, he could find himself on the outside of the family who'd taken him under their wing and given him so much, and no Maisie in sight. Though there was still his old job in the CIB back in Christchurch on offer if he messed up here and needed to get out of town.

Zac swallowed hard and leaned his head back against the seat, trying to focus on where they were going. 'What info do we have on this rescue, Jamie?'

'The man's unconscious, and bleeding from various wounds,' Jamie replied. 'Internally, who knows? It's very likely he's done some damage. The terrain's dangerous with a high risk of boulders falling down the cliff face so we'll have to carry him some distance to where the chopper can lift him out, according to his friend at the scene.'

'What were they doing climbing an unstable rock wall?' Zac wondered.

'We've seen many similar accidents over the years and still don't know what drives people to put themselves at risk. Not to mention the people who have to go out and collect them,' Jamie muttered.

'True.' He stared through the window at the airfield ahead. 'Looks like everything's ready and waiting for us.' The rescue helicopter was warming up, and three other S and R members were standing in the doorway of the aircraft.

'No time to waste,' Maisie said, unclipping her seat belt before Jamie came to a halt.

'Let's do this.' Zac took the heavy, extra medical pack for her, and stood back so she boarded first, smiling at her long legs dressed in fitted outdoor trousers.

No sooner was the door closed, and they were lifting off the ground. Maisie sat beside him, quiet and contemplative. Running through the medical scenario she might have to deal with?

'You okay?' he asked because he couldn't help himself when her hands flexed.

Her smile was tight. 'Yes.' She leaned sideways, away from him, and closed her eyes.

Like she'd prefer to be sitting beside someone else. He hauled in a deep breath, tried to swallow the hurt that created. Now he'd admitted to himself he cared for Maisie as a woman he kept looking for positive vibes coming off her. Not that he was expecting a sudden about-turn from friend to lover when her heart had been broken already. She'd be wary of taking another chance. Just because he was looking at her differently didn't mean Maisie would suddenly come on board.

The chopper rocked up, then down.

The pilot came through their headsets. 'Bit of wind up here, folks. Hope you're all belted in.'

'Hope it improves before we get to the Remarkables,' Maisie muttered.

'It's not going to be much better,' their pilot answered.

Maisie's hands clenched on her thighs. 'Damn.'

Zac tapped her foot with his. 'We'll be fine.'

'I know.' There wasn't a lot of positivity in her voice. 'Why does my fear of heights only affect me in helicopters and not planes?' Her lips pressed together.

'I think that's quite common.' Zac squeezed her hand. He'd prefer to keep holding her, but with these new feelings going on, he didn't dare. Slowly did it. Hopefully.

'Doesn't help, though.' Maisie stared at the floor, her arm against his, getting closer all the time. Leaning into him for strength? Whatever, the sparks were back. Another drop in the sky. Maisie gasped and slid her hand under his arm, nestled against his hip.

To hell with what the others thought. He held her hand. Maisie was scared.

'Sorry about that, folks. I'm going higher in an attempt to dodge the potholes,' the pilot told them.

Maisie remained still, tension rippling off her. 'Why did I volunteer for this?' she muttered. Small dents marked her bottom lip.

His heart squeezed along with his hand around hers. 'Because you're concerned about helping people.'

Because you're tough and caring and always putting others first.

One eyebrow rose and her mouth twisted into a wry smile. 'No getting away from that, is there?'

He nodded, returned her smile. 'Definitely

not.' It didn't stop him wanting to protect her all the time. It was a given in her family. Unlike his. His relationship with his parents had been like living on the other side of the window: able to see in, unable to be seen by the two people who should've been looking out for him. Except when he did something wrong, and then his father knew exactly where he was, showing disappointment with loud admonishments and saying he had to be strong and sensible to get ahead in this world. Mix that with the easy way Maisie's parents treated him and he'd forged a rough line through life with a desire to help others on one side while keeping himself safe from any more hurt on the other. In the few romantic relationships he'd attempted he'd remained on that centre line, afraid to get in deep and be hurt, or hurt the woman he was with. Not to mention the buried feelings for Maisie that had escaped.

Against his arm, Maisie began relaxing and he realised the helicopter was flying without leaping all over the show. He relaxed with her. In this together all the way. As they were in so many things. Hope expanded, filled his chest, made him happy. The possibilities could be endless if he got really close to her—as in as lovers, not just friends. He glanced sideways and felt his gut tighten.

It looked as though she was reading his mind.

Zac swallowed hard. She'd better not be. Too fast, too soon. His gut clenched. His longing was so strong, going slowly might be impossible.

Her mouth tipped upwards in a wry way. So kissable.

He could almost feel her lips under his.

Her smile widened.

Damn, she knew exactly what he was thinking. No, not possible. He knew Maisie.

And she knows you.

Too well, at that. But if she'd guessed his feelings, then she wasn't moving to the other side of the chopper. Or glaring at him as she used to do when she wasn't getting her way. But that had been years ago—when he and Liam had been interfering, bossy brothers who should've kept their noses out of her business apparently. Like the day they'd overheard Beau Coster make lurid suggestions to Maisie and gone in to haul the creep away for a 'chat.' She hadn't thanked them for what she called interfering, said she had it under control. She probably had, but they weren't buying it at the time. 'Feeling all right?' he asked to divert her attention from him.

'Couldn't be better,' she said, still smiling, and confusing him further.

The chopper began dropping height, then hovered. 'This looks the best spot for putting you down,' the pilot told them. 'It's the only flat ground I can see near where you need to be so I'll wait here. You'll have to walk east to find your man.'

'I've got the co-ordinates and this looks fairly close.' Jamie stood up.

Zac slung the medical pack over his shoulders without a glance at Maisie. He liked doing things for her, and didn't want her grabbing the pack off him. 'Let's do this.'

Zac walked beside Maisie whenever it was possible, but mostly they were pushing through low scrub in single file. 'It's not going to be fun carrying a laden stretcher through this.' With six of them they should be able to take breaks if needed.

'Hopefully the man isn't a giant,' Maisie tossed back.

He was average, Zac noted as he spotted the sprawled body ahead with another man sitting beside him. The cliff face towered above them. It was a miracle the guy had survived his fall. 'Hi, I'm Zac. How long ago did this happen?'

'Andy. It was more than an hour ago, likely an hour and a half. Brad's in a bad way. His breathing's all over the place and I don't like how his legs are lying. He slipped and bounced down that cliff.' His head tipped in the direction behind them.

Zac shivered. 'He'd better buy a lottery ticket when he's up and about.' Could be a long time for before that happened.

'I'm a nurse.' Maisie dropped to her knees beside the injured man. Her right-hand forefinger already pressing against Brad's carotid. 'There's a weak pulse.' She was scanning the man from top to toe. 'Brad, can you hear me? I'm Maisie.'

The guy didn't even blink.

Zac got down on the opposite side as Andy scrambled out of the way and delved into the pack for sterile pads and tape. 'That bone looks nasty.' He indicated the right arm.

'I agree. How many splints are in that pack?' Maisie asked.

'Two,' someone answered. 'Need both?'

'Please. I'll check for internal injuries. There's got to be some.' Using scissors, she cut through the front of the jersey and shirt to expose Brad's chest and abdomen. Running her hands over his body, she noted, 'Internal bleeding near the upper colon. And around the liver.'

Zac was taking the pulse rate. He glanced at her. 'Spongy tissue?'

'Yes.'

'Low pulse,' he said, before starting on the breathing rate.

'To be expected. We need to cover that bone, apply a neck brace and splints on his legs, then I'll administer pain relief. He's in a bad way. Jamie, can the chopper come any closer? The less time being carried through the scrub the better.'

'See what I can find out.' Jamie pulled the radio from his belt while moving away.

Zac opened the neck brace and he and Maisie put it in place.

'There's little I can do about the internal injuries.' Maisie placed two sterile pads over the broken bone and taped them firmly in place.

Zac nodded. 'I'll put that arm in a sling to prevent as much movement as possible.'

She gave him a brief smile, her focus entirely on their patient. 'Can you remove a boot? I want to see if he reacts to any touch on his toes.'

They worked well together. Warmth touched

his skin. It felt special. But then any time spent with Maisie was special. 'Spinal damage?'

'Very likely.' She glanced up at the rock wall behind them. 'That would've been some drop with no soft landing.'

'The pilot's going to fly as close as possible.' Jamie had returned. 'But he can't come too near to that cliff or the vibrations from the rotors might bring boulders down on us. He's also concerned that we're in a crevice with not a lot of room to manoeuvre.'

'Safety first,' Zac agreed as he eased a boot off the man.

'Totally.' Maisie flicked Brad's toes.

His foot twitched.

She did it again, harder.

Another twitch, stronger.

She nodded. 'Thank goodness. But we'll still go carefully. Put splints under his legs before moving him onto the stretcher.'

'I'll splint the right leg, but the straightening's up to you.' He didn't have experience of dealing with shattered bones, and the thought of causing Brad pain even when he was unconscious made his stomach churn.

'Fair enough.' Another quick smile came his way, again warming him. He liked her soft smile and the way her eyes widened while looking at him. Did it mean she was suddenly thinking of him differently?

As Maisie worked carefully with the fractured limb a frown appeared. 'I don't want to tear an artery. Brad's got enough internal damage to be going on with.'

'We'll strap his legs onto the stretcher as well.' That'd prevent any movement while they carried him out. Zac took the strap Jamie held out.

Maisie moved nearer Brad's chest. 'Jamie, will you slide the stretcher up to Brad while Zac and I roll him onto his side? Get the stretcher as far under as possible.'

Zac crouched beside her, hands on the man's hip and thigh. 'Ready.'

'One, two three.' They rolled Brad onto his side and Jamie quickly slid the stretcher in place.

With Brad on his back again, Maisie strapped his legs onto the stretcher. 'Let's go. Easy does it as much as possible, everyone.'

The ground was uneven and the scrub whipped back whenever anyone pushed through but the main focus was on keeping the stretcher level and not bobbing up and down with their steps. Everyone was quiet, focused on walking through the rocks and bushes. It was hard going and the men not carrying the laden stretcher did their best to hold back branches or break them out of the way to make it easier.

Maisie walked at the end of the stretcher, keeping a firm eye on Brad. 'I'm pleased he's unaware of what's going on. It would be beyond painful if he was conscious.'

'You would've administered painkillers, surely?' Zac asked as he carried a back corner of the load.

'Yes, but they mightn't be strong enough for this scenario.'

The chopper was hovering, ready for the winch to be lowered. Jamie talked to the pilot as they placed the stretcher on the ground, Maisie trying to protect the patient from the downdraught caused by the rotors.

'You'll be going with him,' Zac noted.

'You're not all walking out, are you?' she asked.

'No, we'll be picked up after you've been dropped off at the hospital.'

'I imagine our man's going on to Christchurch after the local emergency doctors have seen him so you might have a long wait.' Maisie had to lean close to be heard above the helicopter.

Zac breathed in sharply, and regretted the instant that floral scent wafted into his senses. It had nothing to do with the bush surrounding them. Instead it brought dreams, and longing for Maisie, rushing into him. 'Maybe we will start walking, then.' A hard hike would quieten the pounding in his blood, remind him he was supposed to be keeping distance between Maisie and himself.

But it was clearly impossible. He'd adored Maisie since he was a horny teenager, had wanted to get closer in every way, and now... Now he cared for her with all his being.

Except—his chest lifted—what if, when it came to it, he was unlovable? His parents hadn't loved him the way they had each other. His past two relationships had failed because he didn't love either woman enough, was always on edge about how much of himself to give. Becoming vulnerable felt impossible to do. Finally, after a lot of hurt for those women and himself, he'd owned up to himself Maisie was in his system and there was no getting away from her. She did make him susceptible whenever he let her near—so he'd fought to keep his distance. Only now he was ready to face his demons to see if he could be the loving, openhearted man he so wanted to be. If he succeeded, then he might finally accept he could be the father he'd always longed for as a child.

'Maisie, we're sending you up first to un-hook Brad when the stretcher reaches the chopper.' Jamie held the sling out to her. 'Zac, you're after Maisie. That stretcher's heavy and she might need a hand. You can stay on board and hitch a ride back to town while the rest of us slog our way out.'

So much for putting distance between them. But he did like the idea, and the rules said two people had to go with the patient if at all possible in case an emergency arose. So why not him?

Yes. He mentally fist-pumped. *Yes.*

As Maisie was winched up her face tight-ened and lost some of the colour it had re-gained since they'd been on the ground. Zac gave her the thumbs-up and hopefully an en-couraging smile. It was good he was going back with her. He'd be there in case the ride got bumpy. 'No argument from me,' he mut-tered at Jamie's back.

CHAPTER TWO

'HEY, MAIS, I wondered if you might still be here.' Zac stood beside the table in the pub where everyone from the rescue had gathered after being lifted out by another helicopter to wind down over a beer before heading home to their families.

Maisie smiled to herself. Not in a rush to leave—the warmth stealing through her suggested that deep down she must've been hoping Zac might drop by after he'd finished whatever he'd gone back to the police station for—she'd been taking her time over her wine after everyone else left. Maisie saluted Zac with her glass. 'Want to join me?'

Zac made her feel wanted for herself, and as more than a friend. There they were again— new sensations around Zac. Was their relationship changing? Getting deeper? Shifting to a romantic level? Excitement warred with worry. He'd never intentionally hurt her but she understood she didn't always read men correctly when it came to her heart. However, no denying she wanted time with him. Time to get to know him as a man, as someone she might fall for, more than a close friend. As long as they got it right.

'I'll get a beer. Want anything else? Another wine?'

Why not? She could always grab a taxi later if Zac wasn't going back to the apartment block. Except the Zac she knew would drop her off regardless of where he was going. 'Please.' He'd know what to get.

'Pinot Gris?'

Surprised, she named the brand. Since when did Zac ask her what wine she was drinking? Seemed he wasn't taking her for granted. Or she was probably looking for something that wasn't there, because of these new sensations he brought on whenever he was near her. Reaching for her glass she took the last mouthful and sighed. What was going on? She looked across the room and sighed again. No idea, but a tingle of excitement remained whispering in her veins.

Studying him leaning against the counter talking to the barman, she had to admit he was gorgeous. Those broad shoulders filled his jacket perfectly, and his bush trou-

sers might be loose but they accentuated his
muscular thighs causing her own muscles to
spasm. Who was this Zac? Not the guy who'd
hung out with her brother most of their lives.
Not the man who'd tried to talk her out of
marrying Paul and then wanted to help her
pick up the pieces when her marriage crashed
and burned. That man had been the protective
second brother who always wanted to make
sure she was all right and didn't get hurt. A
great characteristic for a friend, even for a
lover, but not when it was overbearing. Once,
when she'd been fifteen and going through a
rough patch over her sister, she'd thought he
was quite the guy. But he'd pushed her away
and she'd moved on. Or had she? She'd never
forgotten how intense he made her feel, or
how her skin used to warm whenever he was
near. Still did, only forget warm, try hot.

With Zac and Liam always in her face she'd
often had to fight them about letting her make
her own choices about friends and hobbies.
There was a day when a boy at school thought
he could walk up to her, grab her to kiss and
grope like he had all the rights in the world.
She'd snarled at him to leave her alone, and
was about to knee him where it hurt most
when Zac and Liam appeared around the corner of the building and grabbed the guy for

a 'talk.' Naturally they were on her side, but she'd been more than annoyed that they didn't give her a chance to deal with the boy herself. How else was she supposed to have become strong?

Gazing at Zac, she smiled to herself. Things were changing. She couldn't fault him. Her feet were itching to dance on the spot, and she fought to remain on her chair. That hunger in his eyes at the wedding had stirred her unexpectedly and she could no longer ignore him and these loving feelings. She was waking up to possibilities she'd buried as a teenager. He had all the qualities she wanted in a man. In a husband. Even as the father to her children. A lover. There was that word again. Wanting him sexually was a new reality that had been growing since the wedding when he'd looked at her with longing in his eyes, and had made her excited to come home to live. Zac was a hunk, no doubt about it. *And* she could trust him not to hurt her.

'Here you go.' A familiar hand holding a glass of wine appeared before her startled gaze.

Familiar but different because these days her body could imagine those fingers on her skin, feel the heat, the passion upping the tempo of her heart. Expanding the need for

him that kept her awake at night too often.
Maisie jerked and her hand knocked over a
glass, fortunately the empty one.

'Careful.' Zac grabbed it as it rolled towards the edge of the table.

She needed a big mouthful of wine but the
way her fingers were shaking she'd only spill
most of it if she tried to lift the glass. Deep
breath, one, two, three, four, five. 'Thanks.'
For what? The wine, saving the glass or for
setting her stomach churning and her blood
warming?

Zac sank onto the nearest stool, watching
her the whole time. 'Are you all right?'

Why was he looking at her so intently? He
couldn't have noticed she was seeing him differently, could he? 'The rescue was full on,
wasn't it?'

'Sure was. You did a great job with Brad,'
he said, as though trying to keep some conversation going on.

He'd be doing a runner if she didn't get
back on track and act normally. 'Everyone
helped, making the whole show easier. And
we worked well together despite it being our
first time,' she added with forced heartiness.
First time working with a patient. Could there
be other, more personal firsts to come? Her
elbows squeezed into her sides. Who knew?

'That's because we read each other easily.' Zac took up all the air and made her feel small beside his long frame.

Another thing she didn't usually notice. Nor did her tummy normally get into a knot just because Zac sat beside her. A hundred things sprang to mind to say, not one of them sane given she needed to stay grounded around him. Risking lifting her glass, she took another mouthful of wine, tried not to choke while hoping to keep this new desire from landing between them, there for ever and never to be taken back. It would create an awkward atmosphere that would change everything. Maisie wriggled her butt on the chair. Everything was changing already. Because she'd started seeing him as a man, not only a friend? 'You're right.' In lots of ways.

'The rescue gave me the same sense of fulfilment I get on the ward. Dealing with the unknown and whatever we find in less than ideal surroundings was great.' Working alongside Zac was an added bonus.

'A good outcome always makes me happier.'

Slowly the tension in her stomach loosened off, and she could breathe evenly again. 'It's all part of fitting back into the community.' But where was she at with Zac? Opening up to these unexpected feelings could mean playing with fire. There was a lot to lose if it didn't work out. For both of them. Another broken heart wasn't happening. She wouldn't recover a second time, especially if Zac was behind it. A lot of dimensions within her family would change, making it hard for either of them to drop by to visit her parents without wondering if the other was there.

'When I returned home from Christchurch after the shooting, I signed up for S and R fast so that I had something to do in my downtime to keep my mind quiet and let it recuperate so I could return to the city at some point, fit and ready to go.'

'Are you ready now?' If he went back to Christchurch what would that mean to her new awareness of him?

'Physically and mentally, yes. Do I want to? I'm not sure.' His gaze was on her, a gentle smile stirring her heart.

So he wasn't rushing away just yet. Good. 'I just want to get on with doing the things I enjoy.' She hadn't had much of that lately, being too busy staying out of the limelight while Paul hit the headlines regularly. 'And settle back into an uncomplicated life surrounded by those who are important to me.' Like Zac.

'Exactly.' He nodded and raised his beer. 'To us and new beginnings.' Then his smile faded as though he'd gone too far. Was Zac having issues about what he was going to do next with his career?

It was too much. She wanted to get back to normal, be relaxed with him. 'Let's go somewhere to eat. My shout.' When he started to reply, she added quickly, 'No argument. If you want to join me, that is.' She might not have much money to her name these days, but she would share what she had.

'Why wouldn't I?' he asked, though there was a hint in his expression saying he didn't know for certain he was being honest. Then he straightened those strong-looking shoulders and gave a teasing smile. 'Here or the Local?'

The Local—real name Queenstown Tavern—was where they'd all hung out in their late teens before everyone disappeared to places yonder. She, Mallory and Kayla on the lookout for cute guys, Zac, Liam and their mates thinking they were the cute guys while keeping an eye out for her and her friends and who they were having fun with. These days the Local was quieter, but still used mostly by regulars. It would be good to go there, and being filled with old memories might help to get these alien feelings under control, if not completely out of her head. 'The Local, of course,' she laughed.

'Good answer.' Dark blue eyes locked onto her, drawing her in, making it hard not to reach for him, to hug him. She didn't usually hug Zac deep and hard, a quick winding of arms around him and that was that, and then only if there was a reason. Yet if she touched him this minute there'd be no letting go for a long time—no reason at all. She shivered.

Zac put his beer aside, unfinished. 'Let's go. I'm hungry.' And suddenly in a hurry to be out of here, judging by the speed with which he stood up.

Taking a long mouthful of wine she set the glass down and joined him, her hand tight at her side to prevent reaching for his to claim back that warmth and strength he'd just removed.

Outside she hesitated, shivering in the sudden chill. The weather had gone downhill since they'd flown back from the Remarkables.

Zac held out the jacket he'd slung over his shoulder. 'Put this on.'

'Don't mind if I do.' She slipped into it, the warmth immediate on her cool skin. The male scent honey to her senses.

'You're not worried I'll get cold?' Finally a smile. A smile that sent more shivers right down to her toes.

'You know me better than that.' Her laugh was tight. Could she be wrong? Snuggling deeper into his jacket, she mulled over the question. How well did they know each other? They'd always got along easily, no doubts about supporting each other and her brother. But—

Then his hand was on her elbow. 'This way.'

'My car's at work.'

'Worry about it later.'

This wasn't Zac's usual easygoing manner. His grip tightened on her elbow, holding her closer to that muscular body that she'd never noticed as anything but as a friend, before, and was now coming to appreciate more and more—*not* as a friend. 'Steady. Don't go tripping over yourself.'

She hadn't even noticed she had. Showed how skewed her mind was. He was just being protective. Typical. No getting away from that side of him. She needed to go home, get away from Zac, but as she opened her mouth she changed her mind. Running away didn't fix a thing, only complicated it further. She was strong. She'd deal with her feelings. Somehow or other she *would*. Starting with being the friend she'd always been, except she doubted that would be easy. She was getting in deeper every time she saw him, even when surrounded by other people. He was someone who wouldn't hurt her, could laugh with without having to prove she wasn't being coy and cute, was able to talk the truth about her feelings.

If Zac knew what she was thinking he'd probably laugh, suggest she got her head seen to. No one just suddenly started falling for someone they'd known all their life. She *wasn't* falling for him. Not at all. These new sensations came out of nowhere, blindsiding her at the wedding. Hands on her waist as they danced, a strong chest under her cheek when they moved slowly to the music. A well of longing and desire expanding throughout her as their bodies moved in unison on the dance floor.

This time she did feel her boot-encased foot trip on the flat pavement and tip her forward.

'Maisie, watch out.' Zac's grip remained firm. And warm. 'How many wines have you had?'

'Two, and don't start going all brotherly on me.' Shouldn't have said that. How else does he think he should act?

His hand tightened on her arm. Disorientating. She leaned closer to prevent another trip on her wobbly legs. And to suck in some of that man smell, to let his hand work a little magic on her arm through the sleeve of his jacket. Zac. Suddenly she felt as though she didn't know him at all. Blatantly untrue, and very bewildering. How could their relationship change after so long? Or had those feelings from her teens been simmering quietly in the background, waiting for her to wise up and move past the fact that Zac and her brother were best buddies and therefore she was almost like a sister to him, and not a woman with needs of her own that included him? But she'd married someone else quite soon after leaving home, which said there was more to these feelings than she was admitting to herself. Had Paul been an attempt to get over Zac? But she'd genuinely cared for Paul at the time, and wouldn't have married him otherwise.

'You're miles away,' Zac noted. 'Care to share?'

'Not really.' Physically mere centimetres away, but he was right. The gap between them was huge. Insurmountable? Only time would tell. Did she want to explore this? Her humming body indicated yes, but her heart was slow. Too much to lose. The pain of getting it all wrong would shut her heart down for ever, reinforcing the fact she wasn't good at choosing the right man. The Zac she knew was everything she hoped for, and usually trustworthy. But that was as a friend, not as a potential lover. He was so sexually attractive, he was becoming impossible to ignore. Becoming? He was already there, sexy as they came. Strange she'd never noticed his wide chest or muscular thighs before. He'd just been Zac, the boy in her life who grew into a man she hadn't really seen, except once as a teenager. Now there was no not noticing him. He oozed sexiness.

'Maisie, if you'd rather go home, just say so.' A crease appeared between his brows, like he was concerned about her behaviour and was about to turn around to head off.

'No way. I'm starving.'

For food, and life, and possibly you, Zac Lowe.

She headed inside. The place was humming, every table in use. 'I haven't been here in years.'

Zac stepped through the crowd, his arm around her shoulders, keeping her close—like he didn't want to let go either. Interesting. 'Let's sit at the bar and see if a table comes free.'

They could eat at the bar but that wouldn't be conducive to talking. Could be for the best though. Enjoy each other's company without getting into deep water. Minutes ago she'd wanted to get away from him because of these feelings, now all she wanted was to be with him. Yeah, he'd got her into a right pickle. She wanted him. She knew that wasn't the best idea she'd ever had. She needed to make up her mind. Go with this and see where it took her and Zac, or back off fast. She hadn't felt this alive and ready for a new adventure in for ever. Not since the police came knocking on the door with a warrant for Paul's arrest and she'd learnt he'd been using her for his own means and that when it all fell down around his feet she'd never really meant a thing to him.

'It's great to be out and about again. I haven't done much socialising lately.'

'So you're glad you came home?'

'Absolutely.'

'I am too.'

More warmth spread through her as she watched him from under lowered eyelids. That angular jaw begged to be touched with her fingers, those lush lips traced with her tongue.

'You heard from Liam this week?' Zac asked as they scrutinised the menus the barman handed them.

Liam? Oh, right. 'He rang a couple of days ago. Said he'd be coming for a visit within the next few weeks. Probably warning me to move out of his bedroom.' She was renting her brother's apartment off him until he made up his mind about buying a house in Christchurch. Somehow he seemed to be dragging the chain about that, and she suspected it was his way of helping her out.

'Think he's serious about this Sasha he's seeing? It's been going on for a while.'

'Haven't got a clue. He's not saying much. As per normal.' Maisie finally relaxed. This was her and Zac, shooting the breeze with no undertones to be heard. It was wonderful.

The only sour point was when she went up to pay the tab and the barman grinned. 'Already seen to.'

'Zac, I said I was shouting,' she growled.

'So you did.' He stared her down with a 'This is what I do' look.

Her heart twisted, and she relented. She rose onto her toes and brushed a kiss over his cheek, barely resisted his lips. 'Thank you.'

What else could she say? It was as if they were on a date. Blatantly untrue, but she'd take it for now.

Zac was laughing on the inside as he drove them back to the apartment block. Maisie had looked ready to read him his pedigree when she learned he'd paid the bill. He got that she was independent and didn't expect him to do that, but that's who he was.

'Since my car's still at work, can you give me a lift to work in the morning?' she asked while staring out the window.

Not liking having to ask for help? That was new. But since Paul she had pushed everyone away when they wanted to help her. 'No problem.' He kept it light, didn't tease her as she'd probably expect. Instead he tapped the steering wheel in time to the music filling the warm air, and breathed deep. Maisie filled him, soft and warm, expanding his heart in a way that was foreign to him.

As he parked in his garage, she turned to him. 'Coffee? At mine?'

'You bet.' Hopping out of the car he raced around to open her door. 'I enjoyed tonight.' It wasn't over, but it also wasn't going to get cosy, or hot, or anything more than friendly.

Not tonight. He needed to get more encouragement before he risked everything.

As she brushed past him her breast touched his arm, and he drew a breath. Friendly that was not. But it hadn't been a deliberate move. There wasn't a lot of space between the car door and the wall so he'd been close, too close apparently. Stepping out into the cool night air, he hauled in oxygen, let his body slowly relax.

She let them into her apartment, charging up the stairs as though trying to put space between them. Her long legs and sassy butt filled him with a need that coffee wasn't going to douse. It would have to. There was nothing else going down tonight.

So find something else to talk about. As he reached the top of the stairs he looked around and smiled. 'You've taken down Liam's favourite painting.' Where the abstract art piece in shades of grey and yellow had hung was now a large black and white photo of Lake Wanaka, waves pounding the shore, whitecaps everywhere, with a lone boat pitching abruptly.

'You honestly didn't think I could live with that hideous picture, did you? If you could call it a picture.' She shuddered, spilling coffee grains on the counter.

'True.' He looked around at what was now a cosy living room with soft pink cushions on the couch and chairs, vases and ornaments filling the shelves. Early irises stood in a narrow straight glass vase on a sideboard. 'This feels right.' A Maisie room. Warm and soft, inviting.

Leaning against the kitchen counter she nodded. 'It's me. I picked up most of the furnishings at the warehouse. It's amazing what you can do with very little to spend. Who needs Rimu tables and chairs, leather sofas?' A hint of bitterness darkened her voice.

'Hey, you've done well. And you're right. This is so you.' He stepped around the counter and reached for her, drew her in for a light hug. Not tight, not too close. Though he was fighting the need to wrap his arms right around her and hold on for ever. 'You're back, and you've made this place your home.'

She'd returned, and he had his old job waiting in Christchurch if he wanted to go back and pick up where he'd left off when the bullet took him down. He hadn't been rushing to go, and now Maisie was here, he was less than enthusiastic. Spending time with her was far more exciting than working every waking hour and then some to solve a murder. But the time for making a final decision was running out. The CIB wouldn't wait for ever. He held her tighter.

They stood there for a moment, quiet together. Then Maisie pulled away, looked everywhere but at him. 'You're right. And I'm happy.'

'Maisie?' If that tone was happy, then he didn't have a clue. 'You all right?'

She turned and locked her gaze on him. Fierce, and determined. 'I'm fine. Truly. Sometimes what happened gets to me, and then I remember it's over and I'm back amongst the people I care about the most in the world.' At last a full-on smile came his way. 'Including you, Zac.'

His heart melted. He could live with that for now. It helped taking things slowly a little bit easier.

CHAPTER THREE

ZAC SHOOK HIS head in exasperation. 'The man's holding the three-year-old daughter of his ex-girlfriend to ransom and I have to play nice.' All the hostage negotiating training Zac had done before returning to Queenstown for a quieter life didn't stop the pain he felt for that little girl he'd heard crying on and off over the last five hours, but he knew how to suppress it and get on with the job. 'Libby's traumatised enough as it is.' Sure, he understood traumatised was better than dead as had been threatened, but sitting here listening to Blake ranting about getting the child's father here was like watching the tide coming and going and nothing changing.

Hooper was at Shanghai Airport waiting for the first flight back to New Zealand and there was nothing anyone could do to get the poor guy here any sooner. Blake had been told so often it was like a record going round and round on the same groove. He refused to budge. Nor would he talk with the child's mother, who was desperate to get her daughter away from the monster.

'You're coping better than I could,' Colin, the station chief, muttered.

'Thanks.' Zac pressed the button on the phone. 'Blake, you need something to eat?' Anything to settle the guy down a little.

'Think I'm stupid?'

Yes, big time. But he was also evil and hurting a little girl. 'Blake, you hold all the aces. I have no intention of using a food delivery to attack you.' Zac rubbed his lower back where a dull throb had set in from sitting so long at the table trying to talk Blake out of his hyped-up scheme of holding Libby until her father turned up. The evil undertone to the man's attitude had the hairs lifting on Zac's neck every time he heard Libby cry.

'What the—?' Blake yelled.

Screams and shouts came from the speaker and through the open windows of the communications van Zac and Colin were sitting in with an internet specialist. Who else was in there other than Blake and Libby?

'Where's Cathy?' Zac asked.

A scream answered him.

'That's Cathy? Inside? How the hell? She's supposed to be with a policewoman.'

'Blake, talk to me. What's going on?' Zac knew he'd be ignored and he'd lost the edge—if he'd ever had one—because someone else had entered the house. It wasn't his battle any more. That belonged to the armed defenders now swarming the building. But he leapt to his feet anyway. He might be able to talk to Blake inside the house, talk him down from whatever high he was on.

'Get out or I'll hurt the kid.' Blake's roar came through the phone on speaker.

'Mummy.' Libby's small voice.

Zac froze. Why had the armed defenders gone in? They must've seen Cathy enter the house from the back, but if so they were supposed to notify him. But he knew from experience how fast these situations could change. How had the woman got in unnoticed? Someone was going to get a speech once this was over, and it wouldn't be pleasant.

'Stay down,' someone snarled. Not Blake so it had to be one of the armed defenders.

Zac waited, every muscle screaming with tension and the urge to rush in to deal to the man who'd caused harm to the little girl. But others were doing that. It wasn't his job today. Damn it.

'Zac, you listening? It's Reed.' One of the armed defenders. 'You're needed in here.'

'On my way.' He leapt out of the van and ran. What now? They must have Blake under control, or something had gone horribly wrong. Heart in throat he raced for the building.

Libby was safe, held in her mother's tight grip as a policewoman escorted them out of the room to the ambulance now parked outside instead of around the corner.

Blake was face down on the floor, cuffed, and spewing vitriol.

'What happened?' Zac asked. 'Why was Cathy in here?' The mother should've been along the road in a police car out of harm's way, not risking harm to her daughter.

'She said she had to go to the toilet and came here instead. She attacked him with that.' An armed defender nodded at the baseball bat.

Great. Did she not understand what could've happened to her daughter if she'd made a mistake? The man was big, she was small. How she'd beaten him was beyond him. But now wasn't the time to say anything. He turned around, stepped up to the man he'd spent the last five hours talking with. Now he could stop being 'nice' and get serious, read him the charges with satisfaction. 'Cut the noise, Blake. It's over.'

Maisie's teeth were grinding as she sponged the little girl's face, removing the smears of tear-streaked dirt plastered to the abrasions on her cheeks and chin. What had that monster done to her? 'There, there, I'm cleaning you up so we can make you better.' They'd be able to fix her physically but emotionally was going to take time and patience from the experts and the child's parents.

Rinsing the cloth in disinfectant, she moved onto Libby's hands, extracting first one and then the other from Cathy Hooper's grip. The mother hadn't let go of her daughter the whole time Maisie had been with them. But then, why would she? It must've been terrifying every second of the hours she couldn't see her daughter, didn't know if she was all right. She'd refused to stay in the emergency department to be treated for her own injuries when Libby was transferred to the paediatric ward. So one of the doctors had come here to stitch up the wounds she'd received when she'd tackled the man who'd abducted her daughter.

'Baby, you're safe now. Mummy's here.'
Cathy's voice hitched with unshed tears.

Libby wasn't saying a word, staring around
as though wondering where the monster had
gone and if he was coming for her again.

Maisie's heart squeezed. Life was so unfair
at times. She'd heard Zac had been the negotiator. He was experienced in these situations
and would've been focused on the task, but
now it was over would he be okay? Did he
need to vent or did he write up the paperwork
as his way of dealing with the event?

The air shifted, and her skin warmed, as
though someone special was near. Glancing
over her shoulder, she smiled her relief. He
was here, and *safe*. No one had been able to
tell her anything more than he'd been the negotiator and had been called to go inside towards the end. 'Zac.'

His shoulder was against the doorframe,
holding him upright. Exhaustion had etched
lines in his face and dulled his eyes. But there
was a hint of relief there too as he fixed on
her. 'Hey.'

It took all her control not to race over and
embrace him. Not that anyone would give
her a hard time if she did, but right now she
had a wee patient to look after who needed
her more. 'You okay?' Silly question. Zac

took negotiations involving children hard because he knew what it was like for a family
to lose a child. His family and Maisie's had
suffered, though with his parents he'd come
on the scene after his brother died from SIDS
and had lived with the consequences.

He nodded. 'Sure.'

Giving him a quick once-over, she smiled,
liking his strength and tenderness. So lovable.
Yikes, better focus on cleaning the torn skin
on Libby's hand, and not Zac. But she was
aware of him, couldn't ignore his presence,
and knew the moment he straightened and
came across to the bed.

'How is she?'

'Sore, bruised, and there are a few abrasions, but no serious injuries.' He'd know she
wasn't referring the mental ones.

How Zac managed to stay calm after what
he'd dealt with was a mystery but spoke tons
about his strength. She couldn't do it. That's
why she was a nurse. She got to care for
the victims of accidents and illnesses—and
abductions—to help try and make them better. She didn't see the anger and rage as it unfolded, and never wanted to, especially after
hearing Zac talk about the shooting that saw
his friend and colleague killed, and put him
in hospital with a gunshot to the abdomen.

He'd taken the hit in an attempt to save the officer in charge. He said he'd done it without thought for the consequences, a reaction, was all. He didn't see himself as a hero, but she did. So did a lot of other people, especially in the police force. 'A good result.'

Zac winced. 'He's off the street, yeah.'

Maisie looked him over. 'Are you sure you're all right?'

'Yes. Got a blinding headache to be going on with, is all.' A crooked smile changed his face.

Ka-thump went her heart. He really was something else. Someone special. Someone who made her want to sing. She laughed. That would have security rushing to haul her outside. Placing her hand on his upper arm, she squeezed gently. 'You're amazing.' Really and truly amazing. Her kind of man. If—*if*—she could risk her heart.

'Don't go all soft on me, or…' He spluttered to a halt.

'Or what?'

'I'll have to take you out to dinner again.'

Now there was a good idea if ever she'd heard one. 'You're on. Now sit down before you fall down.' He was looking wobbly on his feet, now she was studying him as a nurse and not that woman who wanted him in her arms, against her body.

'I need to talk to Cathy for a moment.'

'I'm not leaving Libby.' The woman cuddled her daughter possessively.

Maisie said, 'I suggest you both sit over in the corner, on the other bed, speak quietly so the wee one here can't hear what you're saying but won't lose sight of her mother. She mightn't be saying anything but she can hear very clearly and I'm sure neither of you want to disturb her any more than she already is.'

Dark blue eyes locked on her, glittering with agreement. And amusement at her 'I'm in charge here' tone? Zac conceded, 'You're right. Come on, Cathy. Your daughter couldn't be in better hands.'

Relaxing, Maisie chuckled to herself. He wouldn't have heard her talk like that before. It was strictly a work voice. They were in a two-bed room with no other patient going to be brought in here while Libby was a patient. She'd made certain everyone knew no one was to come near Libby and her mother unless for medical reasons. 'Libby, think you can drink some water for me?' Maisie aimed for distraction to make everything easier on her mother, and to help her stop thinking about Zac's compliment.

Libby's eyes followed her mother the short distance to the other bed, didn't leave her when Cathy scrunched down on the edge and kept her vigil as Mummy talked to Zac.

There was a difficult time ahead for the child and her mother, Maisie sighed. 'Here, Libby, take a few sips.' She held the plastic mug to the girl's lips and urged her to respond. 'That's it. Good girl.' Now for some more cleaning up of abrasions, this time on the legs.

'Want a hand?' Jill appeared quietly at the side of the bed.

Nodding at the nurse, Maisie said, 'Can you bring some fresh warm water and more swabs? I don't want to leave her even for a minute.'

Libby had stiffened when Jill spoke but she hadn't looked her way, remained fixed on her parent, her hand reaching for Maisie's, gripping tight. 'It's all right. Jill's a nurse like me and she wants to look after you too.'

Jill went to get what was needed. When she returned, Maisie suggested, 'You clean those abrasions and I'll keep hold of her hand.' Libby was shaking a little. Time for some food. Though the reaction would have a lot to do with shock and terror catching up. Reaching behind her to the tray on top of the bedside cabinet she picked up a plate with a sweet muffin on it. 'Libby, how about you eat this? Look, it's yummy, with chocolate inside.'

Silently the girl reached out and took the muffin, nibbled at the edge, still watching her mum.

Maisie glanced across to Zac. He wore his serious policeman face but worry darkened his eyes. He must've sensed her looking at him because he turned slightly to look at her, and then at Libby. His fingers touched his right shoulder. Telling her to check her patient's shoulder.

'That's the girl. You'll feel better when you've finished the muffin. It'll make your tummy happy.' Maisie ran her hand over Libby's right shoulder, shifted the neckline of the hospital gown and studied the skin and muscles. Minor bruises, no swelling. Pulling the gown back in place, she lifted her thumb towards Zac.

He nodded once. They were on the same wavelength. A team of two. It would wonderful to take that further. Couldn't be simpler. *Sure.* Just forget the hurt from the past and get on with the future jointly. Love. Marriage. Family. So easy. *Not.* Or was it? Give it a go? Hard not to with her skin heating every time he was near. But easy does it. One step at a time.

Next time Maisie looked across Zac was leaning against the wall, his hands in his pockets, his head dropped forward, staring at his feet. She crossed over, leaving her wee patient snuggled against her mother again. 'Libby's safe. Because of you, the team and her mum. You can be proud of yourself.'

'I am, but now the questions start. Who was responsible for what? How did Cathy get into the house when it was surrounded with armed defenders? That sort of thing.' He lifted his head and stared at her, his baby blues fierce.

Baby blues? Yes, sometimes. And that sparkling cobalt shade when he was smouldering with longing. His eyes were lovely—hot. 'You'll sort it. I know you, remember?' Though obviously not as well as she'd once believed if she now noticed how his eyes had layers of depth and twinkled even when he was serious. 'I bet you wanted to smash the guy to pieces, but you didn't. Instead you did what was required—remained calm and focused.' Her arms tightened, preventing her from reaching for him. That wasn't happening here in the ward where anyone could see them. Jill would tease her relentlessly, as she was always on her back about finding a man to have some fun with.

But she so wanted to show Zac she was here for him all the time as someone special and not so much as the friend he knew. She cared for him in ways that were stronger, and deeper, than she'd felt before. But she had to be careful because if she was wrong, and found she was looking for love with Zac because it was safe and had no real foundation, she'd lose one of her closest friends and that would break her heart even more. She stepped back. 'I'm due a break. Feel like a coffee?'

Her patient was dozing. Jill would keep an eye on them while they went to the canteen.

'Good idea.' He straightened up and touched her shoulder. 'I feel whacked. It's all catching up.'

Heading down the corridor and around the corner away from the ward the need to hug him grew. And grew. To hell with it. This was Zac. Why shouldn't she? Until she'd felt attracted to him she wouldn't have thought twice about it. Moving closer she took his arm, pulled him to a halt and wound her arms around that expansive chest, tight not soft and loose. This was what friends did, right? Even them. But today was different. The faint smell

of aftershave wafted past her nose, making
her shiver with delight.

Zac tensed.

She backed off some. He didn't want her
hug?

Then he was holding her, chin on her head,
his breathing slow and quiet.

Relief warred with guilt. She shouldn't be
wanting to press closer, but trying to stop
the prickles of desire lifting her skin wasn't
working. This was magic. Desire and Zac all
rolled into one. Tensing, she pulled back a
little, instantly regretting it.

Zac dropped his arms to his sides and
stepped back. 'We'd better go get that coffee.'

Her heart sunk. She got the message. They
were *friends*, not lovers, and never likely to
be. Had she given herself away? If she took
a chance on following this desire filling her
more and more often, he still mightn't change
his feelings for her to something so deep it
came with a love that was intimate and loving beyond what they'd always known. This
felt like that day when she was a teenager and
wanting him to hold her. He'd walked away
then too. 'Right.' Not even close, but hopefully he believed her.

Along with Liam, Zac had always been
there for her, since the day Cassey went to

the shop to get ice cream and never came home. It had been an awful time for her family. Zac had felt the pain too. Cassey had been as much a part of his life by then as she and Liam were. It also made things harder for Maisie because the boys became extra vigilant around her. Quiet, shy and more inclined to appease people than argue with them for the sake of it, it became difficult to be strong and stand up for herself with the boys overseeing everything she did. She'd paid them back by becoming the pesky sister always following them around and trying to join in their games, but they never backed off watching out for her. Then she'd started wanting Zac's attention in other ways and he'd shunned her.

As a teenager she'd dug deeper, started working out who she was and what she wanted, trying to ignore what the guys thought best for her. She'd stuck to it pretty much ever since and made some disastrous decisions along the way. But they had been her choices, no one else's. Now, after wrapping up her marriage she was taking a break on being tough, quietly finding her way through life without pushing too hard for anything, being content with what she had. Throughout all the drama of being publicly derided as the wife of someone who could steal from the weak and therefore must've known what was going on Zac was always at the end of the phone whenever she wanted to chat.

Except she hadn't talked to him much about Paul and how he'd decimated her with his crimes and lies throughout their brief marriage. Her family had never cared for Paul, thought he was self-centred, and she'd been defiant about marrying him. She had loved him in the beginning, hadn't seen his ego and need to be wealthy as a problem until it was too late, so the last thing she was going to do was to go looking for sympathy from those who'd tried to warn her.

'Where have you gone?' he asked quietly, his gaze focused entirely on her, his breathing uneven.

She shook her head, giving him a smile. 'I'm here, with you.' In more ways than one. 'Come on. At this rate I'll have to return to the ward before we even get to the canteen.'

Three hours later Maisie parked in her garage and breathed a sigh of relief. The day was over and she could relax, forget about a little girl who'd been put through hell and concentrate on not being a nurse for the next twelve hours. Starting with a hot shower.

Through the lounge window she saw Zac sitting on his deck, head tipped back, and a bottle of beer in his hand. He'd be winding down, letting go the tension from earlier in the day which had probably ramped up at the debriefing he'd gone back to the station for after they'd had coffee in the canteen. Self-contained came to mind. Zac to a T—most of the time.

Turning away reluctantly, she headed for the bathroom and switched the shower on to warm up while she got clean clothes from her bedroom. Jeans and a navy top with green and lemon patterns that opened down to the beginning of her cleavage. Lacy underwear that no man ever saw any more. It was her hidden pleasure. Gorgeous lingerie made her feel feminine and desirable.

Would Zac appreciate her sexy knickers? A bra that opened at the front? What would he think of them on her?

Where did that come from? Turning the dial closer to cold she stepped under the water and gasped. Thinking about Zac and sex twisted her insides and heated places best ignored for now. But a relationship with him would be exciting. This had to be the crazi-est thing she'd ever contemplated. Altering the temperature to bearable, she soaped herself all over and tried to forget what she'd been thinking. But what would she come up with next?

The sight of Zac sitting out on his deck, staring up at the sky—or were his eyes closed and he was thinking about his day?—sucked her in. Made her happier than she'd been in a while. Had her wondering if these new feelings for him really were real, and if they were could she find the courage to follow through?

Damn it. She was going over to his apartment to have a beer with him, and try to clear the muddle in her head. If she really wanted to follow up on these new feelings, then hiding out in the apartment wasn't the way to go about it.

Towelling herself dry she laughed. Wasn't that why she'd got out that particular top and those jeans that hugged her hips and butt like a second skin?

Her phone vibrated on the counter. Liam's name was highlighted.

Heard Zac was negotiator today. How is he? He hasn't answered my messages.

Exhausted when I saw him.

To be expected.

True.

Give him an elbow from me when you see him.

From the day the boys started school together they'd always elbowed each other in acknowledgement of something well done. It had been their way of sharing secrets in front all the other kids.

Will do. Maisie put her phone aside.

Liam hadn't finished. Glad you're there for him.

How'd Liam know she was about to go visit him? Duh. Her brother knew her as well as Zac did. Of course she'd call in on him. She didn't bother answering, instead headed to Zac's apartment.

'Hey.' Zac held his door wide, a startled look on his face as he sussed her out. Never noticed her dressed in fitted clothes before?

'Hi yourself,' she managed around a blockage in her throat. His weather-hewn face was so familiar it shouldn't send the wave of longing ripping through her so that her knees felt weak. Those lips looked so kissable it was just as well her knees weren't able to lift her onto her toes. She'd have made a fool of herself.

This is Zac, for crying out loud.

A man to be relied upon. Sounded boring put like that, because Zac was anything but boring. He was fun and exciting, loved getting out in the bush and on the mountains or in his boat on the lake. And sexy. She winced. She shouldn't have come. 'I came to see how you're doing with getting over your day.'

'I'm fine. Join me on the deck?' He was studying her as though he didn't know her.

Surprise, Zac, you don't. Not where I'm coming from at the moment anyway.

But then she wasn't sure she knew what was going on with her either. 'A beer would be good.' She stepped around him to head out to the deck.

'On to it.'

Maisie sank onto one of the woven outdoor chairs and tucked her legs under her butt. The sun was sinking fast behind the mountains, but the air was still warm. 'Winter will be here before we know it,' she said as she took the bottle Zac held out.

'You ready for snow this year?'

Tauranga had warmer winters and snow was unknown. 'Bring on the skiing. I'll be a bit rusty, but it'll be fun.'

'You never forget the moves. Not when you've skied since you were knee-high to a grasshopper.' Zac tipped his head back as he sipped his beer, his throat exposed.

She looked away, afraid to be caught staring. Her eyes were probably full of lust. Sipping her beer, she tried to find something to talk about. Nothing came to mind.

'How was Libby doing when you finished up at work?'

At least one of them was on track for normalcy. 'The doctor knocked her out with a mild sleeping drug as she got very fidgety and was crying nonstop. Distressing for everyone, especially her mother.' She knew too well from working in paediatrics that being a parent came with a cost. But she also understood how much there was to gain by being a mother.

Paul had been adamant they had to wait until he was established in his career. For once, he got something right, if for wrong reasons. Having the father of her child in jail didn't bear thinking about. Her head turned towards Zac. One day she'd be a mother. When she was sure of giving her heart to a man who wouldn't treat her as badly as Paul had.

Zac would look after her.

Then again, he hadn't done well with his previous relationships, had said he'd always felt uncertain about his ability to love the way he'd seen her parents did. He believed he wouldn't be up to scratch when it came to his own relationships, yet that didn't add up when he'd known nothing but love from her family, and never let them down. But it was probably impossible to forget his roots.

She was learning to trust her judgement, but it had been quite the lesson. Paul's apparent kindnesses came with a price tag. His generosity was at someone else's expense. His need to be wealthy hadn't meant working hard himself; it had been all about taking from those who had. Love hadn't been about sharing their lives and future, hadn't been about raising a family together. No wonder she was reluctant to try again, which meant becoming a mum was way down the track, if it ever happened. Having a child on her own did not feel right for her. She wasn't against women having a baby without a partner, but just not her. Growing up in a loving family had given her strength and kindness that she wanted for her children. She'd be a good mother, but kids needed the balance two parents brought.

Zac's jaw was clenched. Thinking about his day?

She leaned over and gripped his hand.

'Don't. You can't undo what happened, or why it happened in the first place. His day in court's coming and then he'll be living in purgatory.' From what she'd heard growing up with her dad, who'd also been a cop, child molesters and attackers didn't do so well in prison. 'You aren't a violent person so stop even thinking about what you'd like to do because there's no chance you would.'

'Everyone has their point of no return.'

'Yes, and you haven't reached yours by a long way. Don't do this to yourself, Zac.'

His thumb slid back and forth over her wrist. 'We do know each other very well, don't we?'

'We do.' It was how it was, friends growing up, going through their teens and becoming adults and seeing each other's strengths and weaknesses and accepting them. Zac and Liam had a similar relationship. Yet she couldn't help feeling there was more behind what Zac had said than she understood. Nothing unusual there. He didn't always let on about what was really bothering him. After the shooting he initially talked in depth about his pain and anger, but he'd stopped fairly quickly.

Zac crossed to the barbecue and turned

on the hot plate. 'I've got some steaks in the fridge.'

'Want me to toss a salad together?'

'All done.'

'You were expecting me to turn up?'

He grinned. 'What would have kept you away?'

See? No secrets. No surprises. Except she did have one—one she was keeping to herself. She was well on the way to falling for him.

CHAPTER FOUR

'Busy last night?' Maisie asked Faye at swap over. She felt tired before she'd even started work. The few hours she'd managed had been restless. She'd finally fallen asleep as the sun was making itself known coming over the horizon. As she always woke at six regardless of what her day held, she never set her alarm so if Liam hadn't phoned for a chat on his way to work she might still be in bed.

'Fairly quiet.' Faye brought up the file on screen. 'Libby only woke twice and with her mother right beside her she nodded off quite quickly both times. But you'll be getting her up today.'

'The sooner she's moving around normally the better for her mental state too.' Poor little lamb was going to ache all over for a few days from those bruises on her arms and torso.

'Cathy talked a lot during the night. She might not be finished,' Faye warned.

'Letting off steam after a horror of a day.' Maisie got that. She'd been the opposite when she learned what Paul had done. Talking had not been possible. She got too angry, not to mention feeling a fool for ever believing in his so-called altruistic gestures that turned out to be ways of sucking people in to let him take care of their investments so why would she talk about him? Also, at the time, she hadn't known who to trust. Many people, including friends, believed she had to have been aware about what was going on and had condoned it to live a very comfortable lifestyle in a grand house with everything she could want. Yeah, right. She hadn't a clue. Naive and stupid, that had been her. Paul had been a lawyer and made a very tidy income. Coming from an average background she hadn't thought to question how much he made and how they could afford their property. Multiple properties, she found out later as she sat in court listening to the victims' lawyers.

Faye put the file aside. "We had one other new arrival: Debbie Bell, seven, lung infection. She's on strong antibiotics and beginning to recover. No changes with any of the other patients. Harper's still on for discharge after Reed checks him over this morning.'

'That'll make his family happy.' Little

Harper had had ongoing battles with bowel infections since he was one, and this time he'd been taken to Christchurch to have surgery to remove a piece of his colon. He was sent back to Queenstown Hospital a week later, when he was well enough, so his family had more access to visit from their remote farm. 'He's such a cutey, and a stubborn little man as well.'

Standing up, Faye rubbed her lower back. 'I'm going to say goodbye to him and his dad, then I'm out of here. See you tomorrow.'

Maisie nodded. 'Will do.' Taking Faye's place at the desk she scanned the files for details entered during the night. A quiet shift. Since everything was in order she pulled her phone from her bag and pressed Zac's number. 'Hey, how'd you sleep?'

'Not bad considering. You at work?'

'It's what I do.'

'You need a life, Maisie. I'll come up with a plan for the weekend.'

Warmth spread throughout her. 'Sounds good to me.'

He was focusing his attention on her more than usual, and she liked it. 'Liam rang earlier. He says to call when you can. You're a hero at Christchurch PD for stepping between the gunman and your chief to take the bullet.

So don't grump about that. Those guys know how hard it would've been yesterday.'

'I feel good about yesterday.' He knew she'd understand what he meant.

'Great. I'd better go. Talk later.' It would be too easy to curl up and chat the morning away, but she was on duty, and this may be a low-key department but she was the head nurse. That husky voice sucked her in with warm fuzzies.

'See you soon.'

Smiling like a loon, Maisie hung up and went to see her patients.

Straightening his back, Zac stepped into the paediatric ward, scanning the area for Maisie, not the two people he'd come to see, and felt his gut tighten. She was talking to the little boy dressed in outdoor clothes and with a big grin on his pale face, calm and relaxed.

He knew that feeling. Maisie had often calmed him over the months following the armed holdup with her soft voice full of warmth. Once he'd told her the pain his friend's wife suffered, it made him wonder about the people who could be hurt due to a cop's job. Maisie thought he was saying he'd decided not to seek a long-term relationship, but he'd said no. Bad stuff happened everywhere, and that was life, but it had taken time to get past the grief for Benji.

'Don't go chasing the chickens too much for the first few days you're home, Harper. I don't want you to trip over and have to come back here again, do I?'

'I'll be good, won't I, Dad?'

The exhausted-looking man sitting on the end of the bed raised his eyebrows. 'You'd better be.' He smiled.

Maisie ruffled the kid's hair and got glared at for her trouble. 'We're going to miss you but it's best you don't find a way to come back. Stay safe and strong, then you'll be able to help Dad on the farm again.'

She was great with kids and would make a wonderful mum one day. His gut clenched. If he ever accepted fully he could love his own children as the Rogerses had loved him he'd love it for her to have his children. They'd have her pert nose and twinkly hazel eyes, and long legs and—

Shut up, Zac. He took an involuntary step away. *Get a grip or get out of here.*

'Zac? Over here.' Cathy called from the door to the small room.

Zac saw Maisie look around as he headed towards Libby's mother. He sent her a smile before concentrating on Cathy. 'Morning. How was your night?'

'I stayed with Libby, too scared to let her out of sight. I wasn't going to sleep anyway. I can't get the images of Blake swinging Libby from his hand or forget the threats he kept making about what he'd do to her.' Cathy picked at the hem of her rumpled blouse, her eyes full of worry and exhaustion.

'It will take time to get past those pictures.' An image appeared in his head of Benji sprawled on the floor of the liquor outlet, bleeding to death while the gunman aimed his weapon at the chief. Others at the scene had said there was nothing else any of them could've done to change the outcome. The shooter had been out of his head on drugs and nothing would have stopped him from taking the money he'd entered the liquor outlet to steal. But accepting that hadn't been easy for Zac so he'd left the city to return here for a while where life was less frantic and supposedly not as many evil people lurked. He preferred the slower pace and had leapt at the chance to work with the Search and Rescue unit, as if he didn't already have lots to keep himself occupied. Something he had in common with Maisie, if for different reasons. 'Get all the help you're both offered.' The best help he ever received had been Maisie listening to him choke out his anger and pain over the phone. Her support had been fierce, made him strong again.

Cathy ran her hand over her daughter's head, brushing random hair off her face. 'Libby's doing as well as can be expected, I suppose. I don't know what she's thinking, she's still not talking other than to say "Mum" sometimes.'

'She hadn't said anything about what happened?'

'Not a word.'

Zac's heart slowed. The bastard who did this should get locked away for good. But he wouldn't. His sentence might be the maximum time behind bars that the law allowed but it would never be enough. 'What time does her father arrive?'

'In about half an hour.'

'There are more questions we need to ask you later today.' The paperwork had to be done. 'We need to get everything down for the trial while it's still clear in your mind.'

Despair darkened Cathy's voice. 'I can't believe I was so stupid to ever think Blake might be kind and caring.'

'Hey, we all make mistakes when it comes to people in our lives.'

Maisie appeared to stand beside him. 'Don't go blaming yourself, Cathy. It doesn't help, only makes everything worse, and harder to move on from.'

Zac agreed. It had taken him time to let go of the anger from the shooting that took Benji's life and changed the direction of his future. But he wasn't a hundred percent sure that Maisie had got past what Paul had done. Even after the trial judge stated Maisie was as much a victim as anyone else, she'd had to deal with people blaming her for being a part of the embezzlement, if only because she'd enjoyed the spoils.

His heart tightened whenever he thought about that. She never talked about it, other than say she'd made a foolish mistake. Like it was her fault Paul had been corrupt. That she should've seen it even when the detectives who first interviewed him on suspicion of embezzling client's investments hadn't even when they had some evidence to suggest otherwise. It had taken another ten months and four victims before they worked it out enough to prove his guilt. And Maisie had secretly helped them to get the results that put the man behind bars. How could Maisie have done any better? As a detective he knew she'd been in the midst of Paul's corrupt life and should've realised something was out of kilter. As someone who'd known her all his life he understood Maisie was very trusting and believed people for who they presented themselves to be. She'd thrown herself into the relationship with Paul, completely trusted him not to hurt her, and lost so much. Now she was older and wiser, and bruised, that was his Maisie.

His Maisie? Zac stepped back, looked around for a quick exit, taking with him the image of Maisie's gentle yet firm hands helping the young boy. 'I'll come back later.' He needed to get away from her for a bit so he could breathe again.

Maisie, Maisie. She had got under his skin. After knowing her since he was a gawky teen he suddenly felt as though he didn't know her as he'd thought. Certainly not how he wanted to. Even now in a hospital ward filled with sick children she made him long to touch her, to hold her close. To kiss her.

'Zac?' Maisie was behind him, consternation in her eyes.

'Sorry.' He shook his head. 'I just remembered something I've got to do.' Like she'd believe a word of that, but he had to get away. Now. While he still had enough nous left to act slightly sensibly. His feet were already heading along the corridor. 'See you later,' he said over his shoulder. Whether he was talking to Cathy or Maisie he wasn't sure.

He'd see both of them at some time during the day. He had an interview with one and knew there'd be no avoiding the other when she knocked off at the end of her shift. She'd be ringing his doorbell before the day's end like she had last night to make sure he was all right even if he texted her to say he was fine and working. It's what they and Liam had always done for each other and there was no reason for Maisie to stop today. Damn it. He did not want her in his space filling the air with her perfume, rattling his bones with lust, stirring his brain into a mess that said he was seeing her through different eyes and wanting her in ways he was struggling to go slow with. He wanted her, all right, but pushing Maisie could end in disaster. There was only one chance to get this right. Her family were his family, and he owed them so much for the love and consideration they'd always shown him. What if he didn't love her as she deserved?

He'd always protected Maisie, looked out for her, wanted her to be happy. As did Liam, and her policeman father. He was one of the men in her life who'd always been there to make sure nothing terrible happened as it had to her sister. Yeah, and hadn't they all done so well. She'd suffered the consequences of a disastrous marriage, and there'd been nothing any of them had been able to do to prevent it happening—because she'd become so determined to live her life her way without her family interfering.

Damn you, Maisie. You've got to me in ways I'd never have believed possible. How am I going to explain that? To you? To Liam? Your parents? I've ignored my love for so long, pretended it was friendly when I've always wanted you. I'm ready to show you now.

Little did she know he'd been waiting for her to return home one day. Even when he was living in Christchurch he'd waited for the day she'd be back. Now she was here he could no longer deny his love. Nor was he keen to return to Christchurch and the job awaiting him. That'd mean leaving Maisie when he was finally getting closer as a man and not a friend.

What did Maisie think about him? Lately she'd been getting closer physically, as if she wanted more too. Was she open to a relationship?

Damn it, man. Which part of slowly, slowly didn't he get?

CHAPTER FIVE

'WANT TO COME in for a beer?' Maisie called from her front door when Zac climbed out of his car outside his apartment.

He shouldn't. He was exhausted. He'd spent the night tossing and turning while thinking about Maisie—her fingers touching and exciting him yesterday as they walked to the canteen, the tang of flowers as she leaned near, the tightening she brought to his body at the thought of holding her naked in his arms and making love. He wasn't ready to make himself vulnerable to Maisie, but it was already too late. He was defenceless around her. So he should head inside his own apartment and crack a bottle open alone. 'Thanks, but I'll take a rain check.'

'Fine.' Maisie nodded sharply and began to close her door, disappointment blinking at him across the driveway.

He couldn't do it. They were close, no matter how his feelings had changed. He wasn't about to stop being a part of her life. He longed for more of it, not less. 'Maisie, wait.' He strode towards her door, pinging his car locks over his shoulder. 'Of course I want one.'

A tentative smile was her reply, *and* she held the door wider.

Their relationship had changed. Zac suspected Maisie realised it too. Normally she'd have replied with something apt about his attitude and tell him to get over himself but not tonight. Instead she'd looked sad. Which didn't make sense—unless something awful had happened at work today. 'How was your day? Everything all right?'

'It was good.' She headed upstairs to the main living area.

Her jeans highlighted her thighs and butt, brought him out in a sweat. Those same jeans covering that sassy butt had wound him up tight last night and been part of what had kept him awake half the night. His skin began tingling. His mouth dried.

Go home while you can move without having to hide your need.

As if. Too late.

Upstairs he headed straight out to the deck and leaned against the railing to stare across the town below. His right hand tapped the balustrade. Bang, bang, bang. Like the rapid beating going on in his chest, in his veins. He'd always loved Maisie. She was such a part of his life, his being, he couldn't image being without her. Suddenly he was afraid of where this was going. Losing Maisie as a friend wasn't an option. But standing back and not getting involved as his heart needed wasn't an option either. He needed her. He loved her.

The scent of roses wafted around him as Maisie handed him a beer. 'Here, get that into you and hopefully that grumpy face will disappear.'

Grumpy?

Not even close, Maisie.

Confused, uncertain, yes, but not grumpy. He was with the woman he cared too much for. Taking a long draw from his bottle, he changed the subject. 'There's an award ceremony in Christchurch in a few weeks.'

She gaped at him, a silly grin on her face. 'You're up for one.'

'Yeah. Want to come?'

Throwing her arm around him, she planted a kiss on his cheek. 'Try and keep me away.'

'I figured.' Of course she'd be there. She was the first person he'd thought of asking, only he'd been putting it off. No idea why, other than his tumultuous mind that couldn't think straight for any longer than a few seconds. 'Thanks.'

Her grin expanded as she stepped away, leaving him feeling as though some part of him was missing. 'You hear from Liam today?'

'He'll be here Saturday. He's bringing Sasha.'

The new woman. 'That sounds serious.' Liam wasn't known for totting out his female 'friends' for them to meet. Liked to keep his relationships close to his chest. Something he understood all too well now that he'd accepted he loved Maisie.

Maisie swung a bottle of cider in her fingers.

What would they do to his libido tripping over his skin?

'I agree. Not sure I want to hang around in the apartment while they're here,' she laughed, the old Maisie back in play. 'I'll be a spare wheel.' Even though she rented Liam's apartment, her brother still used it whenever he came back to Queenstown. He'd talked about selling it to buy something bigger than his bachelor pad in Christchurch and, if he did, Zac had first dibs. Not that Maisie knew that he was interested in the apartment as part of the property portfolio he was slowly building. If he did buy it, he hoped Maisie would continue renting the apartment from him until she was financially back on her feet.

'You can always stay at my place.' Instantly Zac sucked in a breath, as though he could retrieve the offer. Too late. Anyway, he liked the idea, wanted her to accept.

'Thanks, but I'll go to Mallory's if it gets too much.' She stepped inside. 'I'll get some crisps.'

His shoulders sank. Okay, she wasn't keen to spend too much time with him.

Fight for her, Zac.

'The offer stands. We'll be hanging out with them both most of the weekend and you might need a break.' Having Maisie in the spare room next to his bedroom while he tried to sleep and not dream about what he'd like to be doing with her mightn't be good for him, but he was stepping up.

Following her inside, he closed the door, shutting out the rest of the world, and bringing all his doubts pounding down on his head.

'What's up, Zac? You're all over the show tonight.'

'I am?' Guess he was in a way. He breathed

deep, relished the floral scent that was his Maisie.

'Reliving the hostage situation, by any chance?' She'd returned, packet of crisps in hand, a frown creasing her lovely forehead. 'That little girl and how she was terrified?'

'Not at all.' His hands clenched on the bench in front of him. 'Though now you mention Libby, it was disgusting. Children are meant to be cherished, kept safe.'

Maisie leaned over to cover them with her hands, warm and soft, caring. 'There are some dreadful people out there, which is why you do the job you do.'

'True. But honestly, I'm not thinking about that.'

'If you say so.' Her smile was gentle, full of understanding and something else he was afraid to hope for. Love?

Was it the love he was looking for? Or was it the same love she'd always shown? Love that'd encompass him and maybe their children. All these questions. He was looking for trouble. Breathe. Deep. In, out. In, out. Pulling his hands away from that warmth, he said, 'Sometimes I wonder if I'll ever get up the courage to father a child; I'm so afraid of what's out there that might hurt them.'

Maisie stared at him like he'd just exposed himself. 'You do?' she gasped.

He *had* a longing he'd never put out there before. Might as well follow up or there'd be questions from here to Africa. 'Of course I do. It comes with the territory of being a cop.' That wasn't what she was asking though, was it? 'Yes, Maisie, one day I want to settle down with a wonderful wife and have a couple of ankle biters, and most of the time I accept the fact life's full of dangers for everyone.'

'You've never said anything about wanting to be a dad.'

'Why wouldn't I? I admit to sometimes worrying about how my upbringing might influence how I behave as a parent, but I do know better than that. Your family gave me what mine couldn't. What better example would I want?'

He supposed his parents did love him in their own way, though couldn't they have shown him a little bit? It would've been traumatic for them losing his brother, but Ross and Pippa lost Cassey and still loved Maisie and Liam to bits. They weren't afraid to show and act on it. His parents had worked all hours in their supermarket as though it was a shield from life's problems. They'd been afraid to love him which sometimes made

him angry, sometimes worried he wouldn't
be any better because of the example they'd
set. Mostly he knew he'd been lucky to have
the Rogerses show him differently and that
he could do better.

With a thoughtful look, Maisie pulled back
and reached for her drink.

Instantly he felt something was missing.
Crazy when she was still close enough to
touch without moving off the stool, but there
it was.

'You should never doubt yourself. You've
got a big heart, Zac.'

That heart began tightening as he listened
to the sweet cadence of her voice. Sweet *and*
sexy. Hot. He poured cold beer down his dry
throat.

'You'll be an awesome father. Any kid
would want you for their dad.'

'Only those I have, I hope,' he cracked
through the warmth her words brought on.
'I'm not taking on spares.'

Her smile flicked on, then off. Her finger-
nail began scratching the bench surface.

An ache started under his ribs. Her family
were very protective of her and they treated
him as a second son. Because of that Pippa
and Ross might not like him crossing the line
from friend to lover. Though they knew him,

trusted him. Once again he was getting ahead of himself. 'What about you? Want to have a family sometime?'

Maisie winced. 'First things first. I'm back on my feet, but not rushing to find another man to fill the void. I won't have children without their father at my side.' A delicate shade of pink was filling her cheeks as she stared harder at the view.

'Maisie?' The urge to haul her into his arms was intense. His hands tightened into fists again, pressed into his thighs. He would not follow through on that need. Must not.

Slowly she raised her head and looked at him. 'Zac?'

Confusion tripped out of her eyes, ensnaring him, causing him to wonder what was behind it. 'Are you all right?'

Her breasts rose. 'I'm fine. I thought we were talking about you.' The last words came out on a long sigh.

This hip-hopping from subject to subject was normal, only tonight it felt awkward, as though they were unveiling more depth to their relationship than ever before. Not that either had said much, but that sense of giving away something personal was there. 'I changed the subject deliberately.' He found a smile to make her see he wasn't trying to be a pain in the butt, as she liked to call him.

She turned to face him. 'I'm glad I finally returned home. I missed this, us talking about anything and everything.'

Did you miss me? As in someone to get close to?

'We stopped talking when you got with Paul, remember?' The man had been possessive and jealous and Zac backed away from even the usual friendly phone calls to Maisie to save her any problems. 'Apart from after the shooting when I talked non-stop.' Sort of anyway.

'When I left Paul you kept saying I needed to talk and get it off my chest.'

Zac couldn't help it. His eyes dropped to those beautiful curves filling the front of her shirt.

Maisie hadn't noticed he was distracted. 'It was time to stand on my own two feet and deal with the chaos, the hurt and the public criticism myself. I couldn't hide behind my family or you. I needed to be strong, to grow a backbone, or I'd never trust myself to cope with anything major again.'

Dragging his head upward, he smiled around the lump of longing filling his throat.

'You did that in bucketloads. You've always been tough, going about things quietly, putting yourself out there as a force to be reckoned with. Not saying you aren't, because you always are, but most people don't see that behind the shy face and soft manner.' It was so true even her parents hadn't always seen Maisie for who she really was. Her father and Liam wanted to fight her battles for her and never stopped when she grew up and became a woman. They'd expected the same of him, and to a point he had, while also understanding Maisie needed space, that it was her battle to fight. Maisie had pushed them away, told them to let her sort it out her way for once. And she had.

And he'd gone and fallen deeper for that strong, tough, gentle and no longer shy Maisie. In bucketloads.

'I was seen as selfish in Tauranga. And on the news.' She shuddered. 'It still gives me the creeps to think how a person's life can be exposed so easily.'

He'd spewed vitriol at the screen some nights watching the media having a blast over Maisie's naivety about what her husband had been doing. It got to the point where he couldn't watch any more. Not because he no longer needed to find out what was going on but because none of those reporters knew her and had filled in all the gaps with whatever anyone told them. People who didn't know Maisie, and some who did, had been basking in a moment of glory in front of the cameras.

'I was vindicated with the judge's comments at the trial. There'll always be people who believe otherwise, but...' Her shoulders lifted, dropped. 'That's life and I'm not losing any more sleep over it. Nor do I watch the news very often these days. Can't believe half of what I hear.'

'Onwards and upwards, eh?' Find another man to love and possibly have children with?

Me?

Zac coughed, grabbed his beer and gulped down another large mouthful.

Get over yourself.

Could it be as easy as telling Maisie he loved her with all his heart? He shivered. He was ready. Was Maisie? Did she find him lovable? His heart pounded. Excitement pulsed throughout his body, his head and heart.

'Onwards is enough. You know my head for heights.' A cheeky smile lit up her face and eyes.

Zac relaxed. Or he got close to it. 'Climbing walls not being your thing.' Go for the fun times.

* * *

'Climbing walls and flying in helicopters to name two,' Maisie agreed. 'I still don't know why I let you and Liam talk me into giving that wall climb a crack.' Liam would normally have said no, she shouldn't do it, but they'd had a teenage argument over who was driving Mum's car that day and he was paying her back in typical brotherly fashion. Typically, she'd taken his challenge on despite the fear winding through her. It was a phobia she'd never been able to ignore. That day it had been Zac who'd climbed up to talk her down when she froze twenty metres above the floor in the gym. Come to think about it, it was usually Zac who rushed in to rescue her. A hero. Her hero. If only she could reach across and lift his hand to her mouth, feel his palm with her lips, absorb his heat and strength.

'You were spitting mad at him.' He grinned, sending her heart out of whack. 'I egged you on, thinking you needed to show us what you were made of. I didn't see then that there were other ways to be putting yourself out there in everyone's face to show strength.'

The compliments were flowing tonight. What was Zac after? Maisie chuckled. They weren't kids any more. Even when they were he'd never tried to charm her into anything. So what was this about? It made her feel good—she wanted to get closer. And confused—because she was probably totally wrong about what he was thinking. 'You after something?'

Charm was Paul's middle name. She hadn't seen that in Zac before, but then she hadn't been looking for it either.

'Another beer.' He headed to the fridge.

She kept watching him for something that'd explain why she felt different about him. The man in her kitchen was still the man she'd always known, only now he was exciting, sexier—make that sexy, since she never used to think sex and Zac in the same sentence, not since she was fifteen anyway. That had been buried deep, not allowed out again, though lately there was no denying she found Zac sexually attractive.

His eyes clashed with hers as he turned back. 'You want anything?'

Deep blue eyes, like cobalt metal in the sun. Razor sharp and heart-meltingly enticing. Her mouth dried.

This is Zac, for crying out loud.

Yeah, and hadn't she been getting in a twist about him for weeks now? 'No, thanks.'

Yes, you.

She wanted to know everything. The Zac behind the Zac she'd grown up with. Zac the man. Was this love? It felt different to last time, but then she knew a lot about Zac whereas Paul had been a stranger the day she bumped into him in a grocery store aisle. She'd gone for him, all part of denying any feelings for Zac.

Zac paced to the glass door to stare out at the darkening town beyond.

Maisie's heart rate went sky high. What was going on? This involved her. Don't ask how, but she knew it did. 'Zac? Talk to me.'

Touch me.

Maybe she wasn't alone in being confused about their relationship. Hoping for too much? Was she even ready to pursue that path? To find out what Zac was thinking? These feelings were scary because if she made a blunder by telling him, only to be gently put aside like last time, she'd fall apart. She'd have to leave Queenstown again, go find somewhere else to work and live and get a grip on reality. She could not stay here bumping into him at family and friends' places if she loved him as much as she was coming to believe and not have that reciprocated.

He came to stand in front of her and reached

for her hands. 'I'm heading over to my apartment.'

Her stomach dropped. 'Do you have to?'

'Yes, Maisie, I think I do.' Sadness took the light out of his gaze.

'What's going on?'

His fingers tightened around hers. 'I'm not sure.'

She squeezed back. 'Nor am I,' she whispered and stood up. They were close, not touching but so near her nerves tingled and her heart pounded.

Zac's eyes widened. His breath trickled across his lips and touched her cheek like a caress.

Gentle, drawing her in, filling her with longing so strong it was irresistible. Yet she waited, poised on the edge of change. Her lungs stopped, her heart lay waiting, filled with expectation.

Zac let go her hands.

Her stomach dropped.

Then he took her face in his palms, warm, firm and determined as he looked into her, deep, as though looking for an answer to a question she was uncertain about.

Time stopped. The world stopped. She was with Zac. He was touching her. Searching for something. And she was looking back, holding onto the hope that filled her. Hope they were on this journey together. That she wasn't alone in wanting to move forward together and explore where it might lead. Trying to show she was falling for him.

But what if they got it wrong? Could they go back to who they used to be together? She'd miss Zac in that way as much as losing an arm. He was such a part of her life. Always had been, always had to be. Stepping over the edge was risky—too risky. She stared at him, devouring his strong, beloved face.

He nodded, dropped his hands and stepped back. 'Goodnight, Maisie.'

The door clicked shut quietly behind him and still she stood there, her fingers on her cheeks, tracing where his palms had touched her, where his fingertips had pressed. And tears spilled, washing away any trace of Zac. Leaving her bereft. And just a little relieved because if they got it wrong, then she'd lose too much. She didn't want that. Zac was a friend. Those old loving feelings were back, taking over, and she needed to roll with them. Zac might just be the man for her. But did these feelings come from a sense of safety or were they real and encompassing? Time was required to work through this. Time spent together.

Now what? Could they carry on as though tonight hadn't occurred? What happened to being stronger? Why hadn't she laid her heart on the line by kissing him? A lost opportunity was never recovered.

Slowly sinking onto the chair, she placed her elbows on the metal table and dropped her head into her hands. Tomorrow Liam and his girlfriend would be here and of course he'd see Zac. They were all going for dinner tomorrow night with her parents for starters. Anyway, Zac and Liam were always in and out of each other's apartments whenever they were both here.

Her head throbbed. That look in his eyes wasn't about friendship. It had been deep and sultry, full of longing. The same longing she'd seen at Mallory's wedding. He *was* susceptible to her too. Couldn't they sit down and have an adult conversation about this?

The front door burst open and Maisie's heart soared. Zac was back.

'Sis, you here?' Liam's voice stomped her hope to ashes.

'Sure am.' Her heart thudded. Not Zac. Liam. What if they had leaned in closer and begun kissing? How would that look to Liam if he'd caught them? There'd be all hell breaking loose right now. Liam would never approve of Zac falling for Maisie. He was her second brother in Liam's eyes and that would be gross.

'Howdy.' Liam dropped his arms on her shoulders and pecked her cheeks. 'I finished work early so we decided to change our flight instead of waiting for the morning. Sasha.' He grinned. 'This is my sister, Maisie.'

Maisie's legs were shaky when she moved to greet Sasha, but she drew a deep breath and got on with this development. 'At last.'

Sasha laughed. 'I've been looking forward to coming down here ever since Liam and I got together.' She was relaxed and happy.

So was Liam. Maisie felt a wave of happiness for her brother. It had been a while since there'd been a woman who made him look so at ease, if ever now she thought about it. 'Glad you're both here. Zac's looking forward to catching up too.' He would be, despite tonight's botch-up. 'He's just gone home to get some sleep.' Ouch. He was more likely sitting on his deck contemplating his navel.

'How is he, really?' Liam leaned against the bench. 'Not stressing too much?'

'You know Zac. But he's on track dealing with this case.'

'Figured he would be, but I'll still check him out over a beer. It's been a while since

I was last here and now you all get to meet Sasha.' He hugged his girlfriend close.

Which said she was special to Liam. 'I'm glad.'

Liam got serious. 'Has Zac mentioned the award ceremony coming up in Christchurch next month? He's being recognised for his bravery.'

Maisie nodded. 'Tonight, as it happens.'

Liam was giving her an odd look.

'What?'

'Nothing.' Typical of her brother.

She wasn't fifteen any more. Or twenty. She was divorced and strong, but so not going to ask anything more in case Liam actually came out with something she didn't need to hear. 'Your room's ready.' She used the spare room so that whenever Liam came home she didn't have to move out of his room. 'I'm not being rude, Sasha, but I'm heading to bed. I'm in need of sleep.' Like that was going to happen with the turmoil going on in her head.

'It's fine. I'm feeling weary too. I started work at six this morning so I'd get off early,' Sasha said.

'Right, see you in the morning, Maisie.' Liam looked relieved. 'Unless you're working? Zac's not.'

Bring it on. 'I've got the weekend off.' She

should've put in to work it but she did want to spend time with Liam and Sasha.

And Zac. Definitely Zac, despite, or because of, tonight's fiasco.

CHAPTER SIX

ZAC SCRATCHED HIS stubbly chin. He'd slept in after spending most of the night tossing and turning while his mind replayed holding Maisie's lovely face in his hands. Damn but she was beautiful. Achingly so. Well, he ached anyway. Everywhere. Yep, especially there, where his body needed release. And wasn't getting it any time soon, if at all.

Last night they'd come so close to crossing that fine line running between friends and lovers. So damned near that it suddenly frightened him, made him sit up and look seriously at what he was thinking. But not what he was doing, because close as he'd come to kissing Maisie, he hadn't. Minutes before he'd all but decided to go for it, and then after touching Maisie intimately, staring into those deep hazel eyes and seeing a longing he had not expected, he'd gone and walked away. That need blazing out at him had frightened him, shown how serious this really was—as if he hadn't already known that. Made him realise how easily he could hurt her and get hurt himself.

Mentally Maisie followed him into bed when he got home. Her fragrance, her teasing laugh, her breasts rising and falling when she was agitated, those soft cheeks under his palms. She'd given him a hard-on when she was four apartments away. This wasn't the Maisie he'd grown up with, protected, looked out for, argued with, teased and annoyed. This woman was in his heart, and he'd always look out for her, and probably argue with her, tease her, but now there was so much more depth to those things.

This was Maisie, hot, sweet, strong and smart. Maisie he was in love with. No denying that he probably had been most of his life. He'd do everything possible to make her happy if they got together. But she was more cautious when it came to relationships since her ex's deceitful escapade. No doubt she'd loved Paul, though sometimes she had said maybe she hadn't loved him enough or she'd have forgiven him. Right. Like that was going to happen. The man didn't deserve her.

Putting the kettle on for a strong black coffee, he stared out the kitchen window onto the street. He could go to the station for a bit before Liam arrived. Work was his go-to place when he needed to take a break from things stirring his mind. Most of the week it had been the rescue and the hostage crime, with a little Maisie thrown in. This morning it was all Maisie and nothing else so work would help. His colleagues usually told him he needed to get out more and find a woman to have some fun with.

Guys, I want more than fun.

His previous relationships had been hard work, his heart not totally in them because he'd hidden from his feelings for Maisie. He was just uncertain how to start down the rocky road. If he got it wrong, then Liam and Ross would roast him slowly on the barbecue spit while sipping a beer. Rule one in the Rogers household was protect the women. Rule number two was no different.

His phone buzzed. 'Get your butt over here, man.' Liam. 'The bacon's cooking and I'm about to crack the eggs.'

'When did you get here?'

'Last night. Just after you left Maisie.'

Huh? Liam had seen him and not called out? 'I didn't see you.'

He would've if I'd stayed to kiss Maisie.

Zac's heart thumped against his ribs.

'I figured. By the time I'd parked and hauled Sasha's three-ton case out of the boot and up the stairs I was too exhausted to come find you.' He laughed. 'Get over here so we do the talking with food and coffee going down.'

'On my way.' Relief pounded through his veins. All night he'd been questioning himself on why he hadn't stayed with her since he'd made up his mind to be open with Maisie and show her his feelings. But it had been the need for him in her face that had made him haul the brakes on. Temporarily, he hoped, to give them both time to get used to what seemed to be unfolding between them. And now he was having breakfast with her. Oh, and her brother and his new woman.

'Here, get this into you.' Maisie handed Zac a large mug of coffee. He looked as bad as she felt. Puffy eyes, tired mouth, drooping shoulders.

'Cheers.' He took the mug carefully, not touching her hand. 'You get a surprise when Liam arrived out of the blue?'

'I sure did. He'd finished work early so changed their flight from this morning.' That wasn't what Zac was asking though, was it? If things had gone in another direction their first kiss would've been interrupted and she wouldn't have thanked her brother for that.

Zac was watching her closely, as though looking for her take on last night. 'You all right?'

Smiling wasn't as hard as she'd expected. If they both felt a mess, then they were together on that at least. 'I'm good.' Disappointed and still not quite sure where she was heading with this, but surprisingly, she was okay with it for now. 'You'd better be hungry. Liam's cooking enough breakfast for the whole police department.'

'Typical.' His shoulders lifted a little as he continued watching her. 'Can I give you a lift to dinner tonight?'

Her smile grew. 'Sure.' The four of them could go in one car, but fingers crossed that wasn't suggested by anyone. Time alone with Zac would be just what she needed to get used to allowing her love to come to the fore. Apparently neither was Zac wanting to keep his distance. That had to be good. Bring on more alone time. 'The table's booked for seven.'

'Right, sorted.'

'There you are.' Liam burst into the room. 'Thought you hadn't understood how little time eggs take to cook.' He gave Zac a man hug. 'Looking a bit rough round the edges, mate. Too much off-duty fun going on?'

Hopefully Liam didn't see right through her and recognise her feelings for Zac. Not until she and Zac cleared the air themselves and really got into something deep and meaningful.

'Still working my way through the hostage situation, dotting the *i*'s and crossing the *t*'s so we don't have problems further down the track in court.' Zac looked directly at Liam. No sideways glances to her going on.

'There's someone I want you to meet. Sasha, come and meet the biggest pain in the backside there is in my world.'

Maisie shook her head. Liam was serious about this woman. Heck, if he could fall in love when he'd been such a playboy, then hopefully she could get past her mistake and let love win out. Properly this time, with the right man, the one who'd never hurt her or let her down. Like she'd thought last night, safe? Yes, but not so safe there wouldn't be any fun or excitement. Because with Zac there'd be plenty of that.

Zac hugged Sasha and must've said something about Liam to make her laugh.

Placing plates on the deck table, Maisie listened to Zac interact with Sasha like he'd known her for ever. So relaxed, yet he'd sense Liam's commitment to her and would be sussing her out. Then he looked Maisie's way and grinned as if to say 'not bad.' She laughed. 'Come on, everyone. Let's eat and make the most of the brilliant weather.' It wouldn't be too many weeks before the deck would be the one place she didn't frequent in the apartment with snow covering the mountains and the wind bringing the freezing air to town.

'Winter's on its way.' Zac pulled out a seat for her. 'Then I can take you up to hit the slopes with those skis in your garage.'

'Can't wait.' She rubbed her arms, smiling. 'It's already cooler than it was a week ago.' It wasn't the air making her skin tingle. That was entirely down to Zac. This was new and exciting.

'Who's up for a bit of fishing after breakfast?' Liam asked.

Sasha shuddered. 'No, thanks. I'll take a stroll around town if that's what you've got in mind.'

'I'll join you,' Maisie added. 'I'm not into smelly fish that look at you with their big eyes as the guys knife them.'

'So you won't being eating trout if we catch any?' Zac laughed at her, knowing full well that was one of her favourite meals.

'I might.' She grinned.

'So guys on the lake and women spending money in the shops.' Liam rolled his eyes.

'Couldn't get any better,' Sasha retorted through a smile just for him, showing how close they were.

Maisie's gaze slid to Zac and heat filled her. He was watching her with an intensity that was riveting. Desire swamped her from lips to toes, sending little shivers up her spine.

'You lost your appetite, Maisie?' Liam cut through her daydreams.

Shaking her head, she tugged around to face her brother, her cheeks reddening. 'I wasn't that hungry in the first place.' Not for bacon and eggs.

Zac said, 'We had a big dinner last night, didn't we, Maisie?'

She'd managed some crackers and cheese on her way to bed, and that was it. 'I'm not in any hurry. Sasha and I don't have to be at the shops the moment they open.'

'You don't know Sasha yet.' Liam grinned.

Standing up, Zac said, 'I'll go and sort out the rods and gear.'

'I'll give you a hand.' Liam stood too.

'And leave us the mess to clean up,' Maisie retorted.

Zac leaned his head around the doorframe

and winked. 'Anything to keep you happy, Maisie.'

Her stomach crunched around the little she had eaten. If this was what falling in love with Zac was like, then she was in for a ride and a half. *If* he was in the other seat, and somehow she was starting to think he was, then it would be exhilarating. 'See you later.'

That evening Zac waited at the bar of the restaurant while Maisie popped into the bathroom. Something about checking her makeup which looked perfect to him, especially the mascara that highlighted the gold flecks in her eyes.

'What can I get you?' the barman asked.

'One Pinot Gris and a glass of beer, thanks. Make it the top brand of Pinot you've got.' Nothing was too good for his woman. His woman? There he went again. Leaning his elbows on the bar top, he watched the barman pour the wine, feeling more alive than he had in a long time. It was great to spend time with his mate on the lake, rods out as they talked. Even better being here with Maisie.

She and Sasha had gone into town in the morning after he and Liam left with the boat. Bonding, Liam called it, his voice filled with hope. The relationship with Sasha was serious. No surprise there. It was pretty damned obvious from the look of adoration in both Liam's and Sasha's eyes every time they glanced at each other.

'Another wedding coming up?' Zac had asked. Would this be the third after Mallory and Josue having tied the knot, and Jamie and Kayla about to?

Liam said quietly, 'I think so. You up for best man when I pop the question?'

'I'll give it some thought,' Zac joked around the lump growing in his throat. This was his closest mate talking about marriage. It was great news.

'You do that.'

Spending time with Liam was always good as he missed him now they lived in different parts of the country. They'd always got on well and understood each other. They'd spent the morning on the boat talking about everything and anything—except Maisie—and didn't catch any fish no matter how hard they tried.

'Hey, you look lonely.' Maisie came up beside him.

'Hardly. Just miles away.' Looking at her took his breath away. She was dressed to the nines in a stunning short blue and white dress that clung to her hips and breasts in a very seductive manner. This got harder by the day. 'How was your morning in town?'

'We did a bit of shopping, had a long coffee break, then lunch. Sasha's lovely, and Liam's so happy it makes *me* happy.'

'I got the same message. Another one down, you think?'

Her smile jerked, returned into place. 'I reckon. Zac...' She hesitated.

Wary of what was to come, he stalled her. 'I ordered you a wine. Is that okay?'

'Perfect.' Placing her hand over his and raising the hairs on his arm, she said with no smile, 'About last night. I don't want it hanging between us like a bomb about to go off.' She held up her other hand. 'We're okay today, but it's there, if you know what I mean.'

'I do.' The urge to detonate the bomb was huge.

At last she took her hand away, only to smooth that amazing dress over her thighs, tightening him further. 'You do?'

'Absolutely.' Reaching for the glass of beer as the barman placed it on the counter, he took a mouthful.

'Right.' She sounded disappointed about something.

What had he missed? Was he supposed

to have leapt in and said, 'No, I don't know why I drew away when your mouth was so damned close I ached to cover it with mine, to taste you, to feel you react to me.' Because those were the words hovering on his lips right now. Words that once out there would not be retracted. Nor would he want them to be.

'You're fading out on me.' Her fingers ran across the back of his hand like she was playing a piano.

Playing with fire, more like. Shaking his head, he turned his hand over and held hers. 'Not even close, Maisie.'

Her eyes widened as she stared at their joined hands, and the tip of her tongue dampened her lower lip. 'Tell me. You want to follow up on last night?'

He didn't move, soaked up the warmth for a moment. 'Yes. I do.'

Her gaze turned onto him, and she smiled, a smile that cut to his heart and ramped up hope.

'Evening, you two.' Pippa and Ross cut through the need filling him like a wet blanket.

Maisie slowly withdrew her hand, the heat in her eyes fading just a little.

As was the heat below his belt.

The parents were quickly followed by Liam and Sasha, and everyone was shown to their table looking out at Lake Wakatipu. When Maisie looked to sit between her father and Liam her mother nudged her along to the seat next to where Zac was waiting. It was as though Pippa wanted them to be together.

'What wine are you drinking?' Ross asked his daughter.

Zac gave him the brand.

Ross's eyebrow rose and he looked to Maisie, then back at him, before giving a brief nod. 'Good choice. I'll get a bottle for the table.'

Liam piped up. 'Zac, you spoiling my sister, by any chance?'

Maisie leapt in. 'He knows better than to go for the cheap option when I'm around.'

'Wise man.' Liam grinned.

'I heard you're basically one of the family,' Sasha said to him.

'Absolutely. They all know me too well to be able to get away with anything.'

'Can we have that in writing?' Liam asked.

'I don't think so.' Zac glanced to his side and saw Maisie blush as she turned to talk to her mother. He upped the stakes. 'Naturally I spoil Maisie. It's my way of getting her attention.'

Her hair flicked over her shoulder as her head shot up, that blush deepening. The yellow specks in her eyes were brighter than normal. 'Keep bringing that wine and I'll do anything you ask.' Her next smile rocked him. Again they were on the same page.

So she would've kissed him last night if he hadn't pulled away? Hopefully she'd be willing later tonight if they managed to be alone. He slapped his forehead lightly while wanting to bang his thighs with frustration. Stepping up to the mark, showing his love, shouldn't be full of all these questions. He'd decided to go for Maisie, show her his love, and that meant doing something about it, not worrying about every breath either of them took.

'Anyone looked at the menu yet?' Liam asked.

'We've barely sat down.' Zac reached for his menu, and pretended to peruse it, glad the conversation had moved away from them.

Maisie touched his hand before turning away to her mother. 'When are we going to Dunedin next? I want to get some new jeans.'

Zac stared at the back of her head and thought about how that silky hair would feel running through his fingers. Straight hair that fell to her shoulders, a blond contrast to the blue of her dress shining in the gleam from the overhead lights. His hands tightened as he held onto the yearning gripping him. Now was not the time or place. Reaching for his glass he looked around and found Liam watching him, a cheeky smile on his face. Raising his glass, Zac nodded. 'Set a date soon, will you?' The man needed reminding who'd been talking about marriage that morning.

His friend raised his beer in return. 'You'll be the second to know.'

Zac sighed. If only it was that simple. To be so certain of his future would let him sleep at night again.

'Glad we brought two cars,' Maisie said quietly to Zac when everyone was preparing to leave the restaurant. 'I don't want to be a spare wheel with Liam and Sasha. It's enough to be sharing the apartment.'

'There's still my spare room.' He'd get to spend time alone with her. Another reason apart from driving not to have had more than one beer all night.

Maisie raised her face to look straight at him. 'I know.' Her breasts rose on a sigh.

A knot tightened in his gut. Another near-kiss coming up? He sensed yes was the answer to that too. Near-kiss or go for broke and really kiss her. Deep and long. Learn more about *his* Maisie.

Liam's laughter broke through his day-dream, reminding him that Maisie would probably go back to her bed tonight. He took her hand, then dropped it and took her elbow. 'Let's get out of here.'

Her smile was soft and full of warmth as she slid her hand back into his. 'Let's.'

He didn't break any speed limits but it seemed as though they got to the apartment quicker than usual. Inside he switched on only the kitchen light, leaving the lounge in a soft half-light. While he made coffee Maisie sat on a stool, watching him. Did she feel something for him? He'd never been so in-secure, not even with his parents. She hadn't slapped him down for holding her face and nearly kissing her last night. 'Maisie.' He went around to her side of the counter. 'About last night…' He paused because she was re-garding him with tenderness and something like hope in her face.

'What about it?' she asked when he didn't continue.

'I didn't finish what I started.'

'*We* didn't.'

Her hand caressed his chin. Then his cheek. Then her finger traced his mouth. 'I know I didn't show it, but I didn't like it when you left.'

His lungs squeezed, sending air gushing out. Reaching for her, his hands on her waist, he brought her close to him so he felt her breasts pushing against his chest, her hips touching his, her stomach touching him where he was pulsing. Lowering his head, he placed his mouth on those gorgeous lips and savoured her. Her lips were soft and full and were kissing him back. He wanted more. Needed to taste her, to lose himself in her kiss. His tongue pressed between her lips, touched her heat. His arms wound around her body to bring her into him. This was his Maisie. The woman he dreamed about, longed to know completely. The woman he needed to share himself with. To love and be loved by.

Zac pulled his mouth away. Felt the loss immediately. He stared into the beautiful face so close to his. Maisie. If there'd been any doubt before there wasn't a drop now. He loved her. Totally. She was his life. And he had to protect her. From being hurt again if they got things wrong. But they wouldn't. He loved her.

'Zac? What's wrong?' The doubt and worry in her voice made him drop his arms fast before he could pull her back into his embrace and kiss her senseless.

Stepping back, he rubbed his hands down his face. Like he was trying to remove that kiss. But he wasn't; it was there to stay. 'Sorry, this is tricky.' It was all very well deciding to go forward with Maisie and put his love on the line, but when it came to it, he was afraid of losing her altogether.

'Thanks a lot.' Her lips were quivering. 'I think I'd better go if that's the best you can come up with.'

'Maisie, think about it. We're friends, always have been. I don't want to lose that. Do you?'

'Do we have to?'

'I don't know, and that's why I've stopped. I can't risk it.'

She stood up and took his hands in hers. 'I am going to kiss you. Zac.' She paused, her eyes intense, her mouth soft.

He didn't move for a long moment. His heart was pumping hard, his head light. Everything he wanted was right there, waiting for him. 'The hell with this.' Reaching for her, he lowered his mouth to hers. 'Not before I kiss you first.'

She fell into him as her arms slipped behind his head. Soft, hard, gentle, strong. Her mouth opened under his lips.

The taste of her. Man alive. This was nectar. Maisie beyond his dreams.

The softness of her backside under his hands. Hot, firm, unbelievable.

More than his dreams had ever come up with. More than he could have believed.

'Maisie.' His Maisie.

'Shut up and keep kissing me.'

No problem. It was all he wanted to do right now.

Bang.

'What the…?' Zac jerked back.

'Maisie, you here? I forgot my key?'

Liam Bloody Rogers.

Zac held Maisie to him, not wanting to let her go for a second.

'In my bag by the door,' she called, her hand gripping his waist.

'You guys joining us for a nightcap? Or shall we come up?'

Zac sighed. 'No getting away from them this time.' For once he would've enjoyed telling his friend to go away. 'Come on up.'

Against him, Maisie sighed in frustration. 'Everything seems against us.'

CHAPTER SEVEN

MAISIE'S HEART TRIPPED. The screen on her phone showed Zac. He hadn't been over earlier to spend more time with Liam and Sasha before they left for the airport which had made her uncomfortable. Did he regret their kisses? She'd been steamed up and ready to go where she'd never been before with Zac when her brother interrupted them. Had Liam's arrival caused Zac to rethink what was happening between them?

Zac, who was calling her right now. Deep breath, fingers crossed that he might want to spend some time with her. 'Hello, where were you at breakfast time?'

'Sorry about that but I got called into work. Now I'm ringing around getting the S and R team ready. You available?'

'Of course.' Settle, heart. 'What've we got?'

'A thirty-year-old man has been missing on Ben Lomond since late yesterday afternoon.

Gear up for wind and snow, and possibly an overnighter. I'll pick you up in fifteen.' Gone.

Fair enough. Zac would have others to phone and plans to make.

But her heart was sluggish as she gathered up her outdoor gear and stuffed a jersey and jacket in her backpack. This wasn't getting her anywhere. If Zac wasn't prepared to talk to her, then why had he kissed her in the first place? Like, seriously kissed her as though she meant everything to him. Or was he just a good kisser and she'd fallen further under his spell? No, Zac wouldn't treat her like that. He'd meant every last touch and taste when he kissed her. As she had, returning his kiss with everything she had, everything she felt for Zac, even the confusion about where they were headed.

Filling her water bottle, Maisie focused on the job in hand, because right now that was more important. Someone had been missing since yesterday close to town and the search crew hadn't been called in hours ago? What was wrong with people? This happened more often than she'd realised until she became an S and R member. Someone thought another person would've heard and didn't follow up to find out, and then suddenly urgency flared when it became clear their friend hadn't returned. Hard to imagine what they were feeling now they knew there might be a serious problem with their friend.

This would be her first hike up the mountains on a search. Quietly confident about her walking for many hours and her medical abilities, a vague unease sat in her mind. She was used to tragic scenarios in a hospital with all the backup she required, but out in the wilderness would be different. No fancy equipment, no doctors to make decisions.

Zac's smile when he pulled in with Jamie to pick her up had her toes curling. 'Morning, Mais.'

Happiness swamped her. All was good. She'd been overthinking things. 'Morning, Zac. And Jamie,' she added as an afterthought when he looked over the seat at her.

'The man's friends didn't think anything of it when he didn't turn up for a prearranged dinner last night. Figured he was too tired after his walk up the mountain. It was only this morning when a friend went to see why he hadn't been at breakfast that it was realised he'd never returned from his walk,' Zac told her and Jamie as he drove them to the collection point at the bottom of Ben Lomond. 'Apparently he often goes on walks alone. The problem being he's an Australian from Perth and not used to our mountainous terrain and he wouldn't have recognised that snow was on its way.'

'Didn't people warn him?' It never failed to amaze Maisie how some people went for a walk without first checking out weather conditions which around this area could change from calm to stormy in very little time.

'Seems not. He was heading up the track to the top which, since he's supposedly fit, should've taken four to five hours,' Zac said.

'Next you're going to say he didn't have any food with him,' Jamie said.

'You got it.'

'You've got to be kidding,' Maisie muttered.

'Welcome to Search and Rescue.' Zac tossed her a grin. 'He's not the first, and he won't be the last. How many sandwiches did you pack?'

'More than enough to share around.' She laughed to ease the tension in her shoulders, put there more by Zac's presence than the missing man's situation at this point. 'I presume there's a thermal blanket in the medical kit?' There was one in her day pack if needed, and an extra bottle of water.

'First thing to get packed every time. The

dogs are coming too, though not Shade. Mallory had her at the vet yesterday.'

'She's got an infected foot where she tore a pad playing on the beach.' Mallory had phoned yesterday afternoon, needing a shoulder to cry on since Josue was at work. The baby had colic and wouldn't settle. Shade's problems weren't too bad but Mallory always worried about her pet. They'd talked for nearly an hour with baby Jess crying her lungs out for most of the time while Mallory paced the house.

'What's the plan of attack?' Jamie asked.

'The guy sent photos to a work mate from the top yesterday and mentioned it was getting very windy. We start at the bottom and work our way up, some on the track heading up fast to begin looking around up there while others branch out left and right. Though how anyone could lose their way when the track is very clear is beyond me. It's well marked all the way.'

'I hope he had extra warm clothing,' Maisie thought aloud. 'Otherwise he's going to be hypothermic. Probably will be anyway. That snowstorm might've been short but on the news they were saying it was brutal.' She shivered, thinking about being stranded in that.

Zac pulled in behind other four-wheel-drive vehicles. 'Let's get this happening.'

Maisie followed as he strode across to the group of searchers all dressed in heavy outdoor clothing and strong boots. His head was high and his shoulders back. Zac in action mode. He loved getting out amongst it and helping people, using his skills and knowledge for others. This was happy Zac. Then she shivered. As long as the outcome went well. Not that he'd blame himself if it didn't. They should've been called in hours ago.

'Here's what we know.' Zac rattled off the scant facts, and then put everyone in teams. 'Maisie, you stay with me in case your medical skills are required. We're going up the track to the top with Jamie and Terry and his dog. The guy's name is Martin Cross. Spread out, everyone, and keep in touch.'

Yes. She mentally fist-pumped. More time with Zac. Great. Maisie slipped her backpack on and then lifted the medical kit out of the vehicle. Guess her medical skills were the focus on who she went with and as they were heading straight up to where the chances of finding this man were more likely it made sense. Glad something did, she sighed.

'I'll take that.' Zac reached for the kit, his arm brushing hers.

'I can carry it,' she laughed. 'I'm not a toddler.'

'Maybe, but that's why I've got a large pack—it fits in neatly.' His hand touched hers as he took the strap, sending sparks up her arm. It was as though he couldn't help himself, needed to be making contact.

She got it. They were going to be walking up Ben Lomond together and she was already in a lather about him. Hard not to be when her hands could still feel his muscular shoulders where she'd held tight last night. 'Fine.' She let go her grip on the kit. Arguing over who carried it was a waste of precious time. The most important thing to be doing was to get moving and find the Aussie alive.

Following Zac was hard work. His long legs ate up the ground at a steady pace that wasn't too difficult to keep up with. But just being right behind him and watching how his muscles worked under the fitted fabric of his trousers made her mouth water. It had to be the walking that had her heart beating harder than normal. Had to be. A groan filled with lust escaped her. Okay, maybe not.

Zac glanced over his shoulder. 'You okay?'

'Yes.' Sort of. This was going to be a long day. Unless they found the Aussie in the next half hour. What were the chances? Pretty slim, she reckoned. There were no footprints in what was left of the snow on the track. He had to be above them, or had gone off the track before the snow arrived so any signs of his movements would've been covered during the storm. After a night in the freezing temperatures he'd most likely be struggling to walk down. The best thing he could've done was to find shelter under a tree or bush and curl up to hold in what warmth he could, but people struggled with that concept. Their first reaction was to move, try and find their way out, not realising that made it harder for rescuers to track them down. To remain in one place, alone, hungry, thirsty, frightened, even injured had to be very hard to do, yet it gave people the best chance of survival.

The track widened so Maisie stepped up to walk beside Zac, to heck with not talking. No muscles in sight now which was a bonus for her heart rate. 'I'm picking this guy will be hypothermic.' Hadn't she already said that earlier? 'And possibly injured.'

'Nothing we can do until we find him,' Zac said.

'I get that, and I was just chatting.'

'Sure.' Of course he was experienced in these rescues and wouldn't want to discuss the obvious. He probably suspected she might want to talk about them, and was trying to avoid that.

Maisie slowed to let him go ahead again. Better to watch his legs than talk about the obvious and have him wishing she hadn't joined S and R. Concentrating on where she put her feet, Maisie focused on the climb and tried to ignore Zac. Which was a complete fail. How could she when he was only metres in front of her, striding out while constantly scanning their surroundings? Tall, strong, beautiful. The man of her dreams. He'd always been there, and now this was for real.

Someone to the side of them called out, 'Martin, can you hear me?'

Maisie held her breath, and felt the silence chill her.

After two hours they stopped for a break, sipped water while Zac called up the rest of the search teams one by one to see how they were doing. Everyone was making good progress, but bottom line, there'd been no sign of the missing man.

'Not even a footprint,' Zac muttered as they climbed higher and higher.

Maisie shivered, pulled her jacket sleeves further down around her wrists. 'He's not going to be in good shape.'

'So you keep saying.' Zac elbowed her arm

lightly. 'Try a bit of positivity here, will you?' he added with a smile.

'You're right. He's probably got a fire going and is cooking a rabbit over it as we speak.'

Zac actually laughed, a full happy Zac laugh. 'Hope he leaves some for us.'

Maisie pulled a face. 'I don't think so.' She was besotted with him and still afraid of the consequences if they didn't get it right. Not as tough as she'd thought, huh? Focusing on the track she saved her breath for the walk. Better than saying something that'd change the mood between them again.

Despondency fell over the rescuers when they all congregated at the top.

'No signs of anyone up here on the main track since the snow began,' Jamie said after other searchers had reported negative results.

'Not even the dogs are picking up on a scent to follow,' a dog handler commented. 'Are we sure this guy didn't make it back to town and has left to go elsewhere with no one knowing?'

Zac was wandering along the ridge. 'He's not answering his phone. There could always be a reason for that, I suppose.' He pointed to the far side of the mountain they'd come up. 'Surely he wouldn't have gone down that way? That's the way to all sorts of difficulties for an inexperienced climber.'

'Why would he do that? There are signs showing the track goes back down the way he'd have come up. Nothing indicates a way down to town there,' Maisie said.

'It's possible if he's disorientated,' Jamie said.

'True.' Back to the hypothermia. Or, 'Could he have fallen? Hit his head? Broken a leg and tried to crawl back to the track and lost his way?'

'We won't know until we find him,' Zac said. 'We'll take a break and have some food and hot drinks.'

The day wore on, and no sign of the missing man. Everyone was getting tired and despair was rife.

'Where is he?' Zac growled. 'No one's seen him in town.' He held his phone up. 'His girlfriend's waiting at home for him and she's heard nothing.'

They'd been up and down the mountainside, scrambled over banks and slogged through the long grass out in the open. As the sun dropped behind the ranges everyone met up at a bush hut on the far side of Ben Lomond. 'Take a well-earned break,' Zac told them, while Maisie heated up water for tea and coffee.

Earlier a chopper pilot had flown in pre-cooked food for everyone and it was quickly devoured.

Sitting down beside Zac, Maisie struggled to suppress a yawn. 'I'm going to feel every muscle tomorrow.'

Zac's gaze cruised her legs, up her body and stopped when her eyes locked with him. 'You're doing fine. We all feel it when we're out so long.'

The shiver that rocked her had nothing to do with the chill in the air. The heat in Zac's gaze made her blood simmer while her skin tightened with longing. Not what she should be feeling while out trying to find a man who'd been lost now for more than twenty-four hours. 'I need to get fitter.' And more used to seeing that look in Zac's face.

'Nothing wrong with you.'

My fitness? Or me in general?

Glancing around, she was reminded they weren't alone. So no questions. 'How long will we stop this time?'

'About an hour. We all need to recharge our batteries. We may be fit and agile, but our bodies need nourishing and a rest. There could be many hours walking ahead.' Zac chattered easily now. 'The helicopter's returning around then to use the night vision gear to sweep the mountainside and cover areas none of us have been able to get to. Including the back of the mountain, just in case.'

'I guess there's no such thing as an impossible area when searching for someone like this. The man must be frightened, worried sick about whether he'll make it out.' She couldn't imagine being in that situation. Stuck, alone, lost, maybe in pain. This time her shiver was for the Aussie. 'We've got to find him—alive.'

'We will.'

'That's your go-to, isn't it?' Typical Zac. Positive until proven wrong. Could he apply that to them and their changing relationship? Or could he already have done so, and become worried it could all go wrong, hence his partial withdrawal today?

'What other choice is there?' His grin was a little crooked, his eyes a little darker. 'Probably why I take losing so hard.'

'You didn't lose your last case.' Reaching over she squeezed his hand before withdrawing, hopefully giving Zac something to think about. Something that'd warm him and straighten that grin.

One of the dogs stood up, nose in the air.

'What's up, Boss?' Terry asked.

Woof-woof. Sniff, sniff.

'He's scenting the breeze,' Terry noted.

Zac was instantly alert, hope filling his face.

Everyone was on their feet, looking around, peering through the near darkness.

'Hello. Anyone out there? Martin, is that you?'

Maisie was holding her breath, her lungs beginning to ache. Silence reigned other than the breeze stirring the grass and bushes.

'Terry, give Boss his head,' Zac advised. 'Let's see what he finds. Everyone else spread out behind him.'

Zac called out, 'Come on, everyone. Leave your gear here. If we don't find him soon we'll spend the night in the hut.' He pulled a map out of his pack. 'I'll take another look at the map and see if we're missing something. Though I've done countless searches up here and must know the place fairly well,' he added in an aside to her.

'Every person's reactions to being lost will be different though. What if he's hidden himself for shelter and can't get out again because of an injury? Not easy to find then.'

The quiet night was broken with the thumping of rotors as the helicopter suddenly rose up over the back of Ben Lomond. Everyone paused, watching the movements of the aircraft and where the pilot was concentrating his search. No one wanted to create difficulties by showing up on the second pilot's night goggles.

Zac bent down in a huddle to talk to the pilot on his radio. 'They're going to sweep the steep areas further down the back, leaving the higher inclines to us,' he informed everyone. 'Spread out.'

Torches began lighting up the area randomly, slicing the darkness with sharp beams. Forty minutes later... *Woof-woof.* Boss was sniffing the air, this time in the direction of an area where there was no track.

Maisie moved forward to peer around, picking out bushes, searching their shadows with her torch. Nothing. Boss paced ahead, nose sniffing, head up, and she followed behind Terry. 'Where, boy? Show me.'

They went downwards, across the open grass, towards the bush line, in the opposite direction of the chopper. Behind she heard others talking, saw their torchlight flitting everywhere. 'Hello? Martin, are you there?'

Woof-woof. The dog ran to a bush, stopped and wagged his tail.

Really? Could they have found their man?

A cough. From behind the bush.

'Martin? Is that you?' She ran around the gorse and stumbled to a halt. 'Oh, thank goodness.' A man sat with his jacket wrapped tight around his body, shaking and crying. 'We've found you at last.'

Terry brushed past her. 'Man, are we glad to see you.'

Then Zac was there. 'You're Martin Cross?'

The man nodded, and wiped his sleeve across his face. 'I so happy to see you guys. I thought I was done for.' His voice was hoarse, his body shaking.

Zac pulled out his radio and called the pilots. 'We've found our man. Will let you know what the situation is shortly.'

Maisie dropped to her knees beside him. 'Hi, I'm Maisie and I'm a nurse. Have you hurt yourself anywhere?'

'I think my arm's broken.' He'd tucked the right arm under his jersey.

She'd leave it as it was. Moving it would cause unnecessary pain. 'Did you fall?'

He nodded. 'I think so. Sort of remember sliding down the hill.' His memory wasn't great.

'Anything else hurting?' Maisie took his wrist to check his pulse.

'Just a h-headache, and sometimes I

seemed to forget where I am. I can't believe you found me.' His speech was slurred and his eyes blinking.

'Have you been drinking water all the time you've been out here?'

'I lost my bottle when I fell. I tried m-melting snow in my m-mouth.'

'What about food?'

'A s-sandwich and a-apple y-yesterday when I r-reached the top.'

Maisie turned to Zac. 'Can we have—?' She smiled and took the thermal blanket he was holding out to her. 'Thanks.' *Great minds think alike.* 'Martin, we need to get you wrapped in this. It'll give you some warmth.'

'I've never struck temperatures like they were last night, and today hasn't been much better.' The man gave a weak smile.

Zac had a bottle of water at the ready. 'I'll help you with that blanket,' he said.

'Thanks, mate.'

'What do you think?' Zac asked as she helped wind the blanket tight around Martin's shoulders. 'Anything other than hypothermia and a fractured arm—if it is?'

'I'm treating it as broken for now. He might have a mild concussion.' She'd checked Martin over. 'He moves his legs freely enough, pulse and breathing are normal. I think we can get him to walk to the clearing to be air-lifted out, but I'll be keeping an eye on him every step of the way.'

'I'll let them know.'

'Mostly, he needs to be warm and dry, and get some liquids and food on board.'

'Aka a chopper ride to hospital.' Zac smiled at her. 'The best outcome.'

Her stomach squeezed. 'Yes, definitely.' In lots of ways. They were comfortable together. Sexual tension had come into their relationship and it felt wonderful. As if she'd turned a corner with Zac. This feeling was underlining her feelings and waking her up to how hard it might be to remain uninvolved. She didn't want to walk away from that kiss and the emotions Zac had provoked. She wanted to follow up and have more encounters like that, encounters that led to deeper love and a future. But also, she could never lose him as a friend. Lovers could be friends, but could lovers go back to being just friends if this new relationship didn't pan out?

Confusion almost overwhelmed her. Throw in aching muscles from all the walking she'd done today. Add the relief over finding their man alive and well. Then more relief at how she and Zac had finally gone from cold to warm with each other again, and she was shattered. A hot chocolate and a plate of fries wasn't going to suddenly appear to fix this, but the canned soup and tea back in the hut might go some way to easing the stiffness in her body. A hug from Zac would definitely work to make her feel more comfortable.

'Guess we're up for a night in the hut,' Zac announced to the group after Martin had been airlifted off the mountain. They'd reached the hut where everyone had left their gear. 'Unless anyone wants to walk out now, but I wouldn't recommend it in these pitch-dark conditions.'

Maisie sat down beside Zac with a sigh and leaned against him. 'It's too good to get the weight off my feet to be wanting to walk further now.'

'I should've sent you back on the chopper. As a nurse,' he added when she raised her head to stare at him.

'I wouldn't have gone, so don't go all protective on me. Anyway, there wasn't any room with Lynn on board as well.' The woman had slipped and sprained her ankle as they'd made their way to the helicopter with Martin. Perfect timing, really.

Zac pulled her back beside him. 'Glad you're here?'

'You bet.' She winked. 'So, shall I start heating soup for everyone?'

'Got to get the fire going first,' Zac pointed out.

'On to it,' someone called out from inside the hut. 'We're going to be squashed in on the bunks tonight.'

Zac stood up and reached for both their packs. 'We're in the corner.'

Together? Better than being squeezed between two people she didn't know well. 'Sounds perfect.' Lying next to Zac, maybe cuddle up a bit once everyone was asleep, had to be the best end to a long day. The best they could manage in a hut full of people.

Everyone made short work of the soup and mugs of tea and were soon sprawled out in sleeping bags on the wooden bunks made for six people. 'What's wrong with ordinary bunks?' Maisie asked as she wriggled into her sleeping bag. Not that she was complaining since Zac had scored the two spots nearest the wall. On a regular bunk they wouldn't have been sharing a mattress.

'There's only space for three of those, whereas this way means up to a dozen can fit in,' Jamie answered. 'Crammed as it may be.'

'Lights out, guys,' Zac laughed as he lay down beside her.

The fire was still burning, giving off quite a glow, but hopefully it would die down fast as no one had restacked it once the soup and water had been heated.

Maisie was next to the wall. For once she was grateful for Zac taking over because it meant she didn't have a stranger on that side, and only Zac could touch her or bump into her through the night. How cosy, lying here with him, even though they were in sleeping bags and there were ten other people in the hut.

It got even cosier when the room got darker and Zac wrapped an arm around her waist, snuggled in behind her. His breath was light on her neck where her hair had fallen onto the bundle of clothes that was her pillow. Rolling carefully, she touched his face with her fingers. 'Hey,' she whispered.

'Hey, yourself,' he whispered back.

Along the bench someone was snoring, and someone else muttered, 'Shut up, Harry.'

Rolling onto her back, she laughed softly. 'This reminds me of going camping with my classmates at high school.'

'Who held you then?'

'No one.' She hadn't had a serious boyfriend back then. And Zac had turned her down.

'I probably scared him off,' Zac laughed

not so quietly, raising a growl from the other end of the hut.

Maisie smiled to herself. The first time she got to sleep with Zac and they were in a hut with a crowd. 'We're not very good at this.' If he was going to back off again, then she was going to make it hard for him. Okay, re-phrase that. Make it difficult. There had been longing in his face last night when he'd kissed her. He couldn't deny it. There was longing for Zac in her heart she wasn't going to deny either. They had to follow through and see where they got.

'Roll over,' he whispered. 'I'm going to hold you.'

'Yes, boss.' She wriggled and turned, try-ing not to tangle her legs in the sleeping bag.

'Better believe it.' A light kiss landed on the back of her neck.

Her heart slowed, soft with love. Yes, Zac was the man for her. They had a long way to go to be one hundred percent certain of what they were doing but she was ready to try. Then she tensed. She was still guessing at what Zac felt. Could've got it all wrong.

'Maisie?'

Twisting so she could speak quietly, she asked, 'Is this for real?'

The ensuing silence was finally interrupted by a loud snore.

Her heart thudded heavily. He wasn't answering. She was wrong. She'd have to forget pushing forward. Giving up that easily? No, she wouldn't. No.

'Yes, I think it is.' The words were soft and slow, and purred across her skin.

Relief sighed out of her lungs, and she snuggled closer to that divine body behind her. If only the sleeping bags weren't between them.

CHAPTER EIGHT

IT SEEMED TO take for ever to hike back down to the car park where their vehicles were. Maisie chuckled to herself. Zac thought she didn't realise he was keeping an eye out for her, making sure she was managing now that the search was over. She was feeling a bit flat. Her adrenaline had deserted her after they'd found the Australian, but lying with Zac had made her happy so all in all she felt pretty damned good.

Shoving her pack into the back of his four-wheel-drive, she dug her phone out of her jacket pocket and pressed the number for work. 'Hello, Jill. Sorry but I'm going to be late.' She went on to explain where she was.

'Not a problem. We're not busy yet. Take as long as you want when you get home. I'll call if you're needed later.'

'Thanks. You're a champ.'

'You owe me,' Jill laughed and hung up.

Placing her phone in the console, she clipped her seat belt in place and leaned back to close her eyes. 'I can smell bacon and eggs.' As if. But wouldn't they be great right about now.

'You cooking?' Zac asked.

'Not likely. There's not much left in my fridge after my visitors. I'll grab something at the canteen when I get to the hospital.'

'Unfortunately work doesn't stop because we've been out all night.' Zac turned onto the metal road, heading back to town. That hand that had been splayed across her stomach most of the night was now spread over his thigh. 'You're on day shift, then?'

'Yep. I'll hang around at the end to make up for my late arrival—unless it's so quiet I'm not needed. That doesn't happen often though.' None of them usually walked off on time, mainly because they didn't just finish a conversation with a child or their parents when the time hit three o'clock or whatever shift-finish they had. 'What about you?'

'Depends what's going down, but I usually make up any hours I've missed. I've got a court appearance in Dunedin tomorrow that I need to run through all the details for again, so it's probably going to be a long day for me.' He glanced across, then in the rearview mirror. 'Jamie? You on days or nights this week?'

'Nights, so I get to go home and unwind over bacon and eggs and anything else Kayla might spoil me with.' He laughed.

Maisie had almost forgotten he was with them. She turned to growl, 'You're so mean.'

'I know.' He was smiling.

Facing forward, she closed her eyes again, mainly to stop staring at Zac. She'd got it bad, if she had to do that. Not that it mattered she wasn't looking at him. Her head was full of memories of being held against him, feeling his stomach against her lower back, his thighs against hers, his breath on her neck. And that hand spread wide over her front. Her mouth slipped on a smile. Oh, yes, she'd had a wonderful night and not done much at all. Life was getting better by the day. Make that, by the hour.

Zac pulled up outside the fire station where Jamie's vehicle was parked. 'See you later.'

'S and R training this week,' Jamie reminded them.

She couldn't complain about not having enough to keep her busy, and even better, Zac would be there too.

'I probably won't make it. I'm in Dunedin tomorrow and Wednesday.'

Okay, so Zac wouldn't be at training. She'd survive. This sense of being a part of his life was surreal when they'd always been there for each other but not as a couple.

You're not quite a couple yet.

True. Reality didn't dampen her mood. Happiness had a way of keeping the doom-sayer in her head quiet.

As they drove away, Zac said, 'I can rustle up some breakfast while you're in the shower. It won't make you any later than grabbing a bite in the canteen, and will be tastier.'

She didn't need to rush now that Jill knew what was going on. 'Won't you be late?'

'Do I look worried? The later I start the later I'll leave tonight, that's all.'

She smiled. 'You're on.' Then she yawned. 'If I don't turn up within half an hour I've probably fallen asleep in the shower.' Now there was a thought. Wet skin, warm water, slick hands. *Shut up.* She blushed. This blushing was becoming a habit. Hadn't had a shower with Zac ever. The heat deepened. 'I'll set the alarm on my phone just in case.'

'Damn.'

'What?'

'Nothing.' He swung into their communal driveway. 'See you soon.'

Okay, obviously she was meant to get out fast and not ask what he meant. It was tempting to stir some trouble, but in real life she had a job to get to sooner than later. 'I'll be fast.' But not so fast that she didn't soak away the aches in her calf muscles and back. Or wash her hair to get rid of the knots accumulated from rubbing against her makeshift pillow during the night. She must look like something out of a horror movie this morning, especially once she removed her woollen hat.

'Take your time. I'll grab a shower too before I start cooking breakfast.'

Closing the door before she came out with something about showers and them getting closer, she went into her apartment and dropped the pack on the entrance floor. She'd deal to it when she got home from work.

The plate Zac handed her a while later was laden. 'Get that into you.'

'A full English breakfast. That looks delicious.' Hard to imagine she'd eat even half of it, but she was about to give it a try. 'I'll get the coffee.'

'Sit down. I've got it sorted.'

They ate in a comfortable silence, Maisie barely aware of the time ticking by. She had been told when she started the job that hospital management understood she was a volunteer with S and R and would make certain she could work with both, but she didn't want to abuse their acceptance.

Zac suddenly broke the silence. 'About the award ceremony.'

'I got the feeling you only mentioned it because you knew Liam would say something.'

He swallowed his mouthful and put down his knife and fork, pushed the plate aside. Picking up his coffee, he took a gulp. 'I feel uncomfortable about being recognised for bravery.' She opened her mouth to say something but he shook his head. 'Listen. I know I took the bullet that was meant for the captain, but still, it was a shocking scene with all hell going down. Everyone reacted instinctively. I didn't deliberately think, "The boss's going to get killed so I'll step in front of him and take the knock." It just happened.'

'I guess so.'

'That's it? I'm not going to get a speech?' Relief filled his smile.

'We've been over this enough times for me to know how you feel. It's awesome your bravery is being recognised, and don't argue, you are brave. Others might've kept out of the way and saved their own bacon—instinctively or not.'

'Knew I shouldn't have relaxed so soon. You were always going to have a crack at me.'

He was still smiling though. 'Right, further to that. So we'll be away for the night. I'll book rooms at the hotel the ceremony's being held.'

Shock made her eyes pop wide, and her mouth open. Forget how her heart was reacting. It was going nuts. She hadn't thought about where they'd stay. Zac had said rooms. What about one room to share? 'I can't wait.' Unexpected happiness surged through her. She'd be his partner for the night. *Woo-hoo.* 'Will it be a formal occasion?' A new dress was a must-have. She'd definitely need to go to Dunedin shopping with her mother now.

'Black tie event. I'll have to hire a suit.'

'Hire one? Go all out for once and buy one. Shoes, the black tie, a perfect shirt, the whole works.' Zac didn't go overboard with clothes, more an off the rack kind of guy.

'Now who's being bossy?' He was laughing, like suddenly he wanted to go to this ceremony. With her at his side!

Maisie watched him over the rim of her mug. Sitting beside him at the table, standing up to applaud as he walked up to get his award. How amazing was that? 'Another step in the right direction for us.'

'Are you okay with that?'

'More than okay, ecstatic,' she admitted. 'We are changing, being together in a different way. I'm still not sure where we're headed yet but I'm liking how we're doing.' *And* she knew where she wanted to go.

He suddenly looked floored, making her feel like a spoilsport.

Had she gone too far? Probably, but that was how she tried to deal with problems these days. 'Funny how we've known each other all our lives and yet now I feel I don't know you. Not entirely, or how I thought I did anyhow.'

'Do we ever know a person that well? I doubt it. There must be things a person keeps to themselves, even those they grow up with.'

Talk about the strangest conversation. Could be it was time no matter what went down. Except they both had to get to work. Draining her mug, Maisie smiled. 'As usual, our timing sucks.'

Standing up, he reached for her hand. 'You're right. We both need get out of here and on our way to our other lives.'

Slipping off her chair, Maisie cuddled into him, still holding his hand. 'Thanks for breakfast.'

Zac wound his arms around her, drew her close before lowering his mouth to hers. She pushed up into his kiss, devouring him with her lips, setting her blood humming, her heart banging. She wanted him. Even better, he wanted her. It was obvious in the solid shape pushing into her stomach. When his hands rubbed over her butt, she struggled to remain upright, the need pouring through, her buckling her knees. Who knew kisses could be like this? Not her, for sure.

Pulling back, Zac tucked a stray strand of hair behind Maisie's ear. 'You don't know what you're doing to me.'

Her fingers traced his jawline. 'Oh, I think do, because you're doing it back just as much.'

'How long have you felt this way about me?' he asked.

That was direct. 'For a while. You want a date for when I started noticing you as a man, not a friend?'

'This is an unusual situation to find ourselves in and I don't want either of us to end up regretting anything we might do.'

'I agree, but I want to find out if we're on the right track.'

'How about we date? Go out for dinner, to the pub, for walks, whatever takes our interest, and see how that goes?'

Yes. She mentally fist-pumped. 'Perfect.'

'Can we treat this relationship as though we're new to each other?'

'You're still saying we're not to rush things?'

Like that'll be easy after she knew his kisses were dynamite.

'Something like that.' A wry look filled his face. 'Not saying it'll be a piece of cake to hold off from rushing you into bed, but I don't want to wake up there one morning to find we got it wrong. Know what I mean?'

'Wednesday night when you get back from Dunedin let's go to dinner at Scuzzi's. Might as well start out how I intend to go on.'

Zac stared at her, laughter filling his eyes and lifting his mouth. 'You have changed. Or I never really knew you. Bring it on.' He glanced at his watch. 'And now we'd better get a wiggle on or the bosses will be sending squad cars out to pick us up and deliver us to our respective jobs.'

She brushed a light kiss over his chin. 'See you tonight.'

I know I want you, Zac Lowe, more than I've ever wanted a man before.

Maisie hummed as she drove to the hospital. Not even Paul had rattled her this much. He'd never made her feel as if her world was crumbling inwards into a pool of heat and love, into what her life was meant to be. Something about the serious way Zac'd said they'd start dating more told her he loved her, wanted the whole deal. As did she.

Going on dates would be exciting. It was very different to having a beer at the pub with others or picking up each other's dry cleaning in town. She hadn't dated in years, and could still remember the magic of meeting a man and getting to know him, deciding if there was more to find or it was time to leave. She couldn't see herself ever leaving Zac.

Zac dressed in new navy trousers and a crisp new light blue shirt, then slipped into his black leather jacket, and studied the image in the mirror. 'Not bad.' Hopefully Maisie would be impressed.

Tossing the car keys in the air he caught them and whistled his favourite tune. 'I'm going on a date with the woman of my dreams.'

Maisie took his breath away as she stepped down her stairway to meet him at the front door. Her hair shone under the light. The lime-green dress she wore accentuated every curve and swelling so his heart could barely beat it was so full of need and love. And they were supposed to play good? Not going to be easy, if even possible. But he would because this was the most important thing he'd ever done, making sure they both understood what they were getting into. Love, commitment and family, hopefully with her family's encouragement.

'You look fabulous.' He took her hand and led her outside to the car. 'You know it's a long time since I've been on a date like this.'

Where I'm not thinking just about having a good time and not getting involved.

'Long time since I dated, full stop.'

And she'd broken the drought with him. *Yes.* Opening the passenger door, he said, 'Your chariot awaits.'

She laughed. 'Don't go overboard or I might change my mind about who I'm dating.'

'Not in this lifetime.'

They kept up the banter on the short drive to the restaurant, and then throughout the meal. It was relaxing and fun, and something he hadn't known for a long time. But as they were sipping coffee after their dessert, Zac suddenly asked, 'What do you honestly think your family will think about us being together?'

'They'll be happy.' Hazel eyes were firmly locked on him. 'Why do you ask? No one was glowering at us at dinner.'

'Just wondering if they might be shocked since I've been a part of your family most of my life.' He was backing off, not explaining everything suddenly welling up inside him.

'I'm not buying that, Zac. I understand what you're saying in that we've always been close but that won't stop my family from accepting you as my partner.'

'My feelings for you have changed, become more intense.' So much for holding back. 'Along with that, I worry if we get it wrong, then I'll lose you as a friend, as well as Liam, Pippa and Ross. Just saying.'

Those beautiful eyes locked on him. 'Zac, I'm more than ready to go on this journey together. I'm presuming you want more than a hot fling?'

He reached for her hand, squeezed tight. 'Absolutely. I haven't lied about my feelings once.'

Maisie blinked, then straightened her back. 'You know what? We're adults and make our own choices in life. I don't have a problem with my family and nor should you. I've made stuff up before and still have good relationships with them. The same goes for you. I've been afraid to step across the line and admit how I feel about you, but not any more. I care for you, Zac. A lot.'

A smile began lifting the corners of his mouth and wiping away the frown that had settled on his brow. 'Want to go for a walk along the lake edge?'

'No, take me back to your apartment, Zac.'

His apartment. Zac's heart soared. At the top of the stairs he swung Maisie up in his arms and sought her mouth with his, tasted her, breathed that scent, absorbed her heat.

She was kissing him like she never wanted to stop, devouring him, her lips full and giving, her hands pummelling his shoulders.

Bringing him to a peak, tightening every muscle, heating his blood. 'Maisie,' he groaned between their mouths. He needed to be touching her, *all* of her, learning her body, her needs.

She tore her mouth away, stunned eyes meeting his. 'You're sure?'

Lowering his head, he kissed her like she was his other half. Which she was. Kissed her until he couldn't breathe. Until she melted into him, became a part of him. Then he kissed her some more.

His hand was being wrapped in Maisie's. When had she shifted to be standing in his embrace, her whole body length moulded to his?

She tugged him gently, stepping backwards across the room towards his couch.

'Bedroom,' he gasped.

'Too far.' Hot lips trailed over his chin, down his neck to the vee of his shirt and the skin on his chest. Her free hand cupped his butt, fingers kneading softly.

Keep this up and he wasn't going to last. Lifting Maisie into his arms he strode to the couch and lay her down on the cushions, holding both her hands with one of his to keep her from touching him while he began slowly kissing, tasting, her neck, then the hollow of her throat, following the path she'd been on with him moments ago.

Clothes got in the way. He had to remove some, discover more of that hot, supple body under his fingers.

Maisie tugged her hands free and solved the problem, unzipping her dress, pulling it over her head to toss.

His mouth was dry, his heart pounding as he saw Maisie for the first time. Tanned skin everywhere, full breasts, the dark curls inviting him lower. Lifting his head, he met her steady gaze and fell into her heat. 'Maisie.'

Hands were on his chest, fingers massaging his nipples, sending spears of heat up, down, throughout his body. Lips were caressing his stomach. He was hard, ready. When had he removed his shirt? His trousers were in a pool at his knees where he knelt beside the couch. He stood, stepped out of them and lowered himself beside Maisie. His hands sought her hips, lifted her over him.

Her body on top of him, he slid his hand between her legs, sought her heat, touched, caressed.

She cried out, a loud, long cry. 'Zac.' Then she was shifting, sitting over him, sliding down his length and taking him into her.

His love. Only love. Maisie.

CHAPTER NINE

'I've died and gone to heaven.' Two weeks later, Maisie sighed into Zac's chest as they sat on her couch after making love.

'Hate to disappoint, but I'm just your down to earth kind of guy.' He hugged her tight, breathing in deeply.

'If this is down to earth, then I've been lost.'

'Me too.' Those strong arms tightened around her lethargic body, giving her a heart-felt warmth she hadn't known in a long time, if ever.

A deep yawn rolled up her throat and over her lips.

'What shifts are you doing this week?'

'Day shift for three days, followed by two nights.' Just thinking about running around after sick children made her tired. How did mothers do it when they were feeding babies every few hours and with a toddler requiring attention? Guess love got them through most of the exhaustion, and the sweet moments would be a bonus they'd never forget. Bring it on. She jerked.

'Maisie?'

'Nothing.' Bringing the idea of parenthood into the room now might put an end to the fun. Still too soon for her and Zac. Their lovemaking was beyond wonderful, and they were getting closer all the time, but she wasn't rushing things. She wanted to enjoy what they'd found and let the future unravel day by day.

'You sure?' Doubt lowered his tone.

'Absolutely. I might've nodded off for a couple of seconds.' Now she was fibbing, something she hadn't done since she was a kid trying to get his and Liam's attention. Only protecting herself, and Zac. After all, why spoil another great day?

'Okay, I'll leave you to go to bed.' His breath tickled her neck as his lips trailed light kisses from her ear to the corner of her mouth.

Bed without him? That had only happened when she was working nightshift since they'd first made love. 'I don't think so.' Deep warmth was stealing over her, softening the tightness, loosening her arms around Zac.

She was in a good place, safe and happy, with the man she loved. 'Come here.'

'Oh, sweetheart,' Zac whispered.

Sweetheart? That's me? A smile tripped onto her mouth as she reached for him again. *I'm Zac's sweetheart.*

Words that stayed with her at work a few hours later as she nursed seven-year-old Courtney after an appendectomy.

The young girl had been brought into hospital about four that morning and been sedated until the local general surgeon arrived from Wanaka where he'd been for the weekend. Now she was starting to waken and needed to be watched in case she became distressed.

'You look shattered,' Jill commented from the next bed where a girl was lying with her broken leg held above her body. 'Have a fun weekend?'

'Absolutely.'

'I saw you at the pub with Zac Lowe last night.'

'Where's Mum?' Courtney was awake.

Thank goodness for little girls, Maisie thought as she turned back to her patient. 'Your mum's waiting in the next room, Courtney. I'm Maisie, and I'm looking after you for a while.'

'I want Mummy.'

'In a few minutes we'll shift you to a different room and then you can see her. Can you sip some water for me?' Maisie held the plastic cup and placed the end of a straw in Courtney's mouth. 'That's the girl.'

'Why am I here? I haven't got a tummy ache any more.'

'The doctors took your appendix out, and they gave you something to make the pain go away. I'm going to see how your pulse is now you're awake.'

'What's a pulse?'

'Feel here.' Placing Courtney's finger on her pulse, she asked, 'Can you feel that going bump, bump?'

The girl nodded. 'What is it?'

'That's your heart pushing the blood around your body to take food and water everywhere. Right, that's all good so we can go back to the ward now.'

Meg, Courtney's mother, stood up the moment the orderly pushed the bed out of recovery. 'Hello, darling.' Turning to Maisie, she asked, 'Is she all right? The surgeon said the op went well but I don't want her in pain.'

'She's receiving a light painkiller and antibiotics intravenously and everything's normal. It's just a matter of taking it quietly for the next couple of days and then she'll be running around as per usual.'

'And I'll be wishing for something to shut her up.' Meg smiled. 'She's usually such a busy soul, I struggle to keep up with her.'

'Better that way than moping on the couch all day,' Maisie said. Kids should be active and spend a lot of time outside in the fresh air.

Thinking about children again, Maisie.

Why not? If what she and Zac had going already, then it was a natural process. Love, lovemaking, babies. Holding their baby in her arms, against her breasts. Oh, yes. Her breasts ached at the thought. So much for taking things slowly. Here she was taking giant leaps, acknowledging he'd be a wonderful father, loving and caring. Her heart flipped. He was her man. She adored him. He made her feel good about herself again. Like she was floating on air all the time. Her confidence was back; she was in charge of her life and sharing it with the man of her dreams. Her trust issues were gone. Happiness was there when she woke in the mornings, stayed with her all day, went to bed with her every night.

So who would their baby be like? Tough and dark haired with big blue eyes like his or her father? Or dark blond and slight like her? Intense and out there like Dad? Or shy and non-confrontational like Mum? Boy or girl? Yearning filled her, swamped her heart. Her hopes were lifting all the time, her worries about losing a friend apparently gone. Her love for Zac was real and deep, and she felt safe giving him her heart. She didn't want safe any more. She wanted to leap from the clifftops, shouting her love to the world.

'I'm hungry.' Courtney broke into her thoughts and reminded her what she should be focused on.

'You can't have too much yet as your tummy's got to settle down. You chat with Mum while I go and see what I can find in the fridge.' There wouldn't have been anything from the kitchen delivered at breakfast time for this one as orders were put in the night before. Yogurts and fruit were kept in the staff fridge, along with cereal and sometimes bread in the cupboard for these circumstances. In the kitchen she put on the kettle for a coffee as her break was due, then retrieved a yogurt and banana for Courtney.

'Here you go, my girl.' Fingers crossed she ate these foods. Picky eaters weren't so easy to cater for around here.

'Yum.'

Phew. 'Right, while you eat that I'm going

to have something to eat too. I'll see you shortly, okay?'

'She's coming right fast,' Meg said.

'They usually do, but be aware the after-effects of anaesthesia can make her drowsy on and off for the rest of the day. She might also feel nauseous, though the way that yogurt's disappearing I doubt there's anything out of order with her stomach.'

Meg chuckled. 'I hope you're right.'

'Want a coffee?' Maisie asked Jill as she went past the desk where she was working on the computer.

'Sure do. Be with you in a minute.'

Grabbing her phone from her locker, Maisie checked to see if she'd missed any messages. Heat warmed her cheeks. Zac had texted.

How's your morning going? We've got four burglaries to sort out. Could be busy tonight. Be in touch.

Okay, not quite what she'd expected. That was a normal Zac message, not one filled with xxx's. Guess he was focused on trying to track down the bad guys.

Chugging along. Missing you. Xx

Only being truthful, not over the top. Disappointment hovered in her mind. This was getting out of hand. She was overthinking things just because Zac's message hadn't been filled with love and kisses. Dropping the phone back in her bag, she shut her locker and went to make coffee. Jill always had plenty to talk about after a weekend and she could do with the distraction.

Jill poked her head around the door. 'We need to get ready for two five-year-olds. Knocked off their bikes by a van which didn't stop. Injuries include fractures and abrasions.'

Maisie's stomach tightened as she rushed after Jill. Not quite the distraction she'd hoped for.

It had been a hectic week with long hours culminating in the arrest of three men responsible for stealing to-order high-end televisions and music systems from across the South Island, and Zac was happy to be out on the water with Maisie. He idled the motor while she dropped the anchor off Glenorchy. 'Give it a few metres extra,' he called. Too short a rope made for uncomfortable swinging.

Maisie flipped him a finger. 'How many times have I done this?'

Often. 'Don't want to spoil our picnic bobbing around.' He grinned at her cute derriere sticking out from the front of the boat. He had been looking forward to this downtime with her for days.

A slight hand covered his and twisted so that the motor stopped. 'You going to stand there all day? I'm looking forward to fish for dinner.'

Now there was a challenge if ever he heard one. 'Wait and see.'

She delved into the chilly bin for two bottles of water and handed him one, then made herself comfortable on one of the seats. 'This should be fun. I prefer rainbow to brown trout, by the way. And I'm not helping when you land it. Yuk.'

He shook his head at her as he lifted his rod and checked the fly was secure. 'You want to catch your own?'

'No way. I'm quite comfortable doing nothing, thanks.'

She looked it too, and gorgeous in fitted black jeans and a thick merino jersey the colour of her eyes. His heart did a little skip. Everything was perfect. The sunny day and the calm lake, the easy camaraderie between them, knowing they were becoming closer as a couple—yes, perfect. As long as he caught a trout.

As Zac was about to admit defeat an hour later he felt a tug on his line and raised his rod sharply. 'Got you.'

'You've got one?' Maisie stood to peer over the edge of the boat. 'Want me to get the net ready for when you bring it to the surface?'

'Good idea.' He was winding, then pausing to give the fish its lead, winding again. Slowly, slowly did it. He'd lost enough to know the score. And today he really wanted to put dinner on Maisie's plate. It was a big trout.

'Not bad,' she told him. 'Allowable size anyway.'

He'd have swatted her backside for that if he didn't need two hands to bring in his catch. 'Get ready with that net.'

And don't take it from the mouth end, he nearly added, but she already knew how it worked. Knock the hook out of the mouth and there went dinner. The fish leapt out of the water, splashed down again.

'That's more than takeable.' He grinned, winding in the loose line.

'I know.' Maisie held the net just above the water, ready to scoop as soon as the trout reappeared. It was right there.

'Now.'

She already had it and was lifting it onto

the boat. Then she high-fived him. 'Great going.' She got him a low-alcohol beer from the bin. 'Your reward.'

No, that'd be seeing her face fill with pleasure when she ate dinner tonight after he baked the trout. 'Might as well set up lunch now that I've done what I came to do.' He broke down the rod, dealt to the fish and cleaned up the deck.

Maisie opened the picnic hamper and unpacked the food. 'Oh, yum, my favourite pasta. And ciabatta. Marinated mussels.' She gaped at him. 'Spoiling me by any chance?'

'Why wouldn't I?'

She nodded. 'Can't think of any reason.'

They were on the same page—again. Happening a lot lately. He couldn't remember being so happy. Sitting down beside Maisie he took her hand in his. 'We're doing okay, aren't we?'

A frown formed on her brow. 'Stop looking for trouble, Zac. Everything's wonderful.'

She was right. His ingrained fear of hurting Maisie and losing everything was a pain in the butt. Once, when he was sixteen and still angry at his parents for not loving him how he expected, Ross had told him his anger was pointless, and he should put his energy into doing the things he could. Ross had been his mentor, and usually right, but he'd also made certain he and Liam kept an eye out for Maisie. Zac had never been able to let that go. He owed Ross and Pippa for their big hearts at a time they were suffering for Cassey. But he owed himself a life too, and they'd be the last to tell him otherwise.

Sipping his water, he looked at this woman turning his world upside down in ways he'd never imagined possible. He was lucky to have her, to know her and be able share parts of himself he didn't usually do.

A loud roaring sound began penetrating his consciousness, getting closer and louder all the time. 'Someone's in a hurry,' he noted as he saw a speed boat barrelling across the water half a kilometre away.

Maisie stood up and stared across the water. 'Hope he knows what he's doing,' she muttered. 'There are other boats anchored where he appears to be heading.'

Apprehension flickered in Zac's gut. The boat's speed was sending out big waves behind the craft that would rock the other boats hard. 'Look out,' he yelled, knowing he couldn't be heard. 'I think we need to—'

An almighty crash shook the air, and the sound of metal impacting on metal rang out across the water. 'I'll pull the anchor, you start the motor,' he told Maisie. 'Someone's got to be injured for certain.'

She didn't waste time talking, went straight to the control panel and, after checking the gears were in neutral, switched the key. Then she quickly packed up their meal and put the chilly bin up the front of the boat out of the way.

'Go,' Zac called as he stowed the anchor and hooked the lid in place.

The boat moved forward, and Maisie increased the speed a little. The sooner they got to the scene the better for anyone in the water, and at the speed she was doing, they weren't going to create waves and add to anyone's distress.

'You take it,' she said when he stood beside her. 'I'll keep an eye out for anyone in the water.'

Another boat had pulled anchor to make their way closer to the accident. The speedboat had come to an abrupt stop, its nose high out of the water with a gaping hole on the underside, and the engine half submerged at the back. The small launch it had run into was on its side and two heads were bobbing in the water, alongside the boat.

Zac slowed right down and scanned the water between them and the launch. 'I'm going to them first. See anyone with the speedboat?'

'Not yet. Hang on. There's someone floating face down. Left, Zac, left, that's it. You're on track, pull back on the throttle. Stop, we'll float the last bit.' Maisie was doing up the life jacket she'd just pulled on. 'I'm going in.'

'No, Mais. I'll go. You could get caught up in something from the boats.'

Too late. She was over the side and in the water, making for the incapacitated man.

'You're supposed to stay safe,' he growled. She'd have swiped at him if she'd heard.

Zac left the motor idling and went to stand on the flat space beyond the deck where it would be easiest to bring the man on board. Definitely a male by the width of the shoulders and the short hairstyle, though that might be being sexist.

Maisie reached the guy and immediately began turning him over. She struggled and Zac dived in, swam across the small gap to help. Between them they rolled him over, and began dog-paddling back to the boat, pulling him along between them.

'Hello? Can you hear me?' Maisie asked. She was looking at his head, then down his upper body. 'He's unconscious which suggests he breathed in water without knowing.'

Zac climbed onto the boat and grabbed hold of the guy while Maisie did the same. 'This isn't going to be easy.' There wasn't a lot of space between the large motor and the edge of the boat. 'I'll take his shoulders and try lifting while you see if you can pick up his legs when I get them a little way out of the water.'

Maisie held onto a welded pipe with one hand so she could lean out ready to grab the trousers when Zac pulled the man up and back into the boat. He began pulling, lifting, doing whatever it took. His lungs began burning with the effort, his legs shaking with strain, and still he hadn't got far. He took one step back, pulled.

'Got him,' Maisie yelled as she leaned further forward.

Don't fall in.

He fixed his gaze on the man coming further into the boat, inch by long inch, until suddenly he was tripping backwards as Maisie lifted the legs over the side into the boat. 'Done,' Zac grunted, drawing in a lungful of air.

Maisie was already kneeling on the deck beside the guy, tilting his head back, listening for breathing. Then she rolled him on his side and banged his back.

The man gasped and spewed water everywhere.

'Hello, can you hear me?' she asked.

Shocked eyes opened, stared at her.

'You've been in an accident and ended up in the water face down,' she explained. 'I'm going to keep you on your side in case there's any more water in your lungs. Understand?'

A short nod.

'How many were on your boat?' Zac asked. He hadn't seen anyone else by the speedboat but with the speed the accident happened someone else could easily be in the water and some distance away.

'Just me,' the guy croaked.

'I'm going to take a look around and see if the others by the launch are all right,' Zac told Maisie. 'I'll go very slowly so as not to cause waves or rock the boat. Okay with you?'

'Yes. I'll check this man over.' She was fingering the skull wound. 'Can you feel pain anywhere else other than your head?' she asked her patient.

The man coughed and more water appeared from his mouth. 'I'm not sure. Everything feels odd.'

'Explain.' She sounded so calm.

'My sight's blurry. Sharp pain in my chest. Something's happening.'

Maisie reached for wrist. 'I'm checking your pulse.'

The man tried to sit up.

'Stay still.' Maisie's hand splayed across the man's ribs, keeping him down, while with her other one she found his pulse.

'Chest hurts,' he repeated.

Zac was keeping an eye on the water, flicking looks at Maisie and the man, and calling the emergency services. 'I've got the ambulance service on the line.'

'Tell them we need the rescue helicopter with a medic.' She didn't look away from the guy.

After passing on her request, Zac put the boat into neutral and picked up the handpiece for the marine radio. 'Queenstown marine, this is Zac Lowe. Come in.'

'Marine base, Zac. What's up?'

'There's been an accident offshore at Glenorchy and people and boats are in urgent need of help.'

'Help's already on its way.'

'Zac,' Maisie called. 'He's having a cardiac event.' She was tearing the shirt from the man's chest. 'He's arrested.'

'Cardiac arrest. Inform the rescue helicopter crew,' he yelled into the handpiece before dropping it and going to Maisie's aid. Kneeling down he took the man's head and tipped it back to open the airway.

Maisie was pressing hard into the exposed chest with her interlocked hands. 'When I say, give him two breaths of air, then sit back while I do compressions again.'

'Tell me if you want a break from the compressions,' he told her.

Sweat was beading on Maisie's forehead. Doing CPR was no picnic, but Maisie was handling it like a pro, which she was. The man didn't know how lucky he was to have a nurse on hand when his heart conked out.

'Two breaths.' She nodded.

One, two. Zac sat back on his haunches, holding the man's head again.

Push, push, push. Maisie had a steady rhythm going.

Gasp. Cough. Water spilled out of the man's mouth as Zac hurriedly turned his head sideways.

'Yahoo, well done.' He grinned with relief.

'We're not out of the woods yet,' Maisie warned, but she was smiling. Tugging a roll of paper towels that was tucked into the side panel of the boat, she wiped the man's mouth and then face. 'He's been sweating and I didn't notice, just thought he was soaking wet from being in the water.'

'No one would've thought differently,' Zac said. The man's clothes were drenched, as was his hair and skin.

'What's the story about the helicopter?' Maisie asked, her finger on the man's pulse.

'I'll find out.' He scrambled to his feet.

As Zac made the call, he looked around and saw that other boats were with the launch the speedboat had hit. No one was panicking so hopefully that meant no other serious injuries and Maisie wasn't needed, because she had her hands full. She couldn't leave this guy to go help someone else.

'The helicopter's on its way, should be about ten minutes away,' he was informed. 'The pilot wants you to head to shore at Glenorchy where people are waiting to take the man off the boat to the helicopter when it lands.'

'Will do.' Zac filled Maisie in. 'That work for you?'

'Definitely.' She smiled at him. 'Well done, partner.'

Partner. His heart squeezed. Raising his thumb in acknowledgement, he said through a wide smile, 'We make a good team.' In so many ways. He was giving it everything, no more doubts or holding back or worrying about what could go wrong. Ready to take a chance on being together for ever. 'A great, loving team.' He turned the motor on.

'We sure are,' she agreed.

Zac couldn't believe how happy he was. The days were brighter, the nights warmer. Maisie was the only woman he'd truly loved, and now that he was putting it out there for her to see and be a part of, it felt wonderful. Something he'd longed for all his adult life was coming to fruition. Better still, she reciprocated by being loving and exciting. She had his back, even when he didn't need it, sensed his needs almost before he was aware of them. Stuck up for them as a couple whenever he voiced concerns over her family. She gave herself to him, trusting and open, not trying to prove to him she was as good as him as she'd done for years. He couldn't ask for anything more.

'There you are.' Maisie's soft voice caressed him as she approached him at his dining table from the top of his stairs.

Nice pants. Tight enough to accentuate those shapely legs and not look like she'd squeezed herself into something two sizes too small. Sexy came to mind, and tightened other parts of his body. 'Hello, gorgeous.'

She kissed him before pulling out a chair opposite. 'The rescue chopper brought in two teenagers from Coronet Peak this morning. They'd been racing down the slope and lost control. Severe injuries for both.'

'I heard the paramedics had been called out. What were they doing up there? There's not enough snow for snowboarding yet.' He should be used to people behaving idiotically by now, but he wasn't.

'A lot of people are asking the same thing, but then teenagers being what they are, there probably won't be any sensible answers.'

'I remember those days. Liam and I doing donuts in the car on the back road and wondering why we got caught.'

'Because Dad was a local cop you got a bigger telling-off than most and made to do community service for a month.' Maisie was laughing. 'But you never did it again, did you?'

'Actually, we did, but we went somewhere no one would find us so it wasn't as much fun. Deflating, really, so your dad won that one.' And a few others he wasn't going to mention. 'At least I'm tolerant of teens these days. Hope I'll be the same with my own.' Most of the time.

'Why wouldn't you be? You'll want to make up for your parents by being the best dad out there.'

That stumped him. Her lovely eyes were underlining her statement, showing she meant every word. His heart was slamming. He was lost for words.

'Only saying it as I see it.' Her mouth curved into a gut-wrenching smile.

He needed space, time to absorb her belief in his ability to be a good parent. 'So what brings you here? I thought you were going to see Mallory after work.'

'I'm on the way, just wanted to drop in to see you first.' Now she eyed him up as though there were other things going on in her head.

Things he didn't want to hear about because he was already getting hot for her. He sighed his frustration.

'Problem?'

'All's good.'

I love you, Maisie. How do I tell you that? Are you ready to hear it? We're getting on so well, but—

The old 'but' scenario. And he'd thought he'd buried it. Most days were free of doubt. Damn, he needed to move on, grow a backbone, do something more than go round in circles.

She knew him better. 'I can see that.' Sarcasm wasn't usually her strong point, but being wound up about this made her sound like she was asking too much of him.

He didn't do sharing when it came to his emotions, especially love. 'Drop it, Maisie.'

A soft hand touched his arm. 'If that's what you want, but, Zac, we're becoming a couple, we share more than ever.' She paused, obviously waiting for him to agree.

He did, and then again there were things he couldn't share yet. Once said it would be out there, and if Maisie didn't love him as he did her, then this was over. He wasn't ready for that. Would never be ready.

Her hand disappeared. 'I see.' She stood up. 'I'm obviously wrong. I don't have a clue what's going on here, but I'll leave you to get on with whatever you've got planned and go visit Mallory.'

He'd gone and done the one thing he was desperate not to—hurt her. Leaping to his feet, he reached for her. 'I'm sorry. I've been getting wound up about things and took it out on you.' Leaning closer to brush a kiss on her mouth, he found himself kissing air as she stepped back.

'Not so fast. What's bugging you? Us? Our relationship? It can't be work because you usually talk to me about that.'

The problem was Maisie knew him too damned well. But she didn't know he loved her.

'I see.' She spun away and headed for the stairs.

No, you don't.

He went after her, his gut in knots. What if she walked away and that was it? 'Maisie, stop.'

She did, turning to eyeball him. 'I'm listening.'

'I get nervous about us and what's happening. It's such a huge change in our relationship I worry sometimes about what lies ahead.' He didn't tell her he loved her, he showed it. Didn't he? Possibly not, if she was unaware. 'You've been hurt before. I don't want that happening again.'

One shapely eyebrow rose slightly. 'You believe I don't have moments where I pause to take a breath? Don't wonder about this and where we're headed?'

Of course she would. It was in her make-up to wonder if she was doing the right thing for others, and herself. He'd slipped up there. 'I'm an idiot. It's just that you seem so relaxed about everything and I've been reluctant to burst the bubble by expressing my concerns.'

And my love.

'That's not how relationships should work. Not for me at least.' She bit her bottom lip. 'I don't want a repeat of my previous marriage. We have to talk about what bothers us.'

He took her hands in his. 'I'm not trying to hide anything, Maisie. It's all happened so fast that I have to keep pinching myself to see if it's true.'

Doubt crossed her face, disappeared again. 'You're worried I might get cold feet?'

'Not at all. When you give yourself, you give everything.' It dawned on him that's how she'd been with Paul, which only made what the man did all the worse. And him suddenly more cautious. Was he seriously good enough for Maisie to love? He hadn't been for his parents. They hadn't been able to love him without hesitation. It was different with Maisie. The sane side of his mind knew that. But the doubts from his childhood knew when to creep in with their negativity. He'd hate for Maisie not to love him as much as he loved her.

'Not quite so much any more,' she admitted, squeezing his hands. 'I might've toughened up, but I'm wary of putting myself on the line now, even with you.'

'I get that. I have the same thoughts.' Watching her, he saw the moment she relaxed and let him off the hook—for now anyway. 'That's why we were supposedly going slowly.'

'We don't know the meaning of the word.' Her face softened and a small spark came into her gaze. 'I suppose knowing each other so well complicates falling in love in unexpected ways.'

Thump. Falling in love. Was she in love with him? His hands jerked, then relaxed in hers again. Of course he loved her and wanted the same in return, but what if she woke up one morning and found she wasn't ready? Or had made a mistake and this was a rebound moment?

Maisie pulled her hands free of his.

She was going to leave, go to Mallory's.

Then she slid her arms around his neck and reached up on her toes to place her mouth over his. 'Relax, Zac. It's early days. But forget slow. It ain't happening.'

His body agreed, every part of him roaring into life, crying out for her, obliterating his concerns in an inferno of need.

He hugged her tight. 'This is why I care for you so much.'

CHAPTER TEN

'HANDSOME DOESN'T BEGIN to describe you,' Maisie said as she straightened Zac's bow tie. Her stomach was doing its washing machine number on her, and her fingers wouldn't stop shaking. This was Zac's big night and she would be there, right at his side, and the excitement levels kept growing as the time to head downstairs to the hotel's conference room and the awards dinner approached way too fast.

'Then what does?' Zac teased. 'And don't say I should wear an evening suit all the time.'

'I think you should.' The black suit and crisp white shirt turned handsome into mouthwatering, stunning and sexy as it was possible to get. 'I've never seen you look so suave. Every woman in the room will want you.' They'd have to fight her for him first.

'I'm not the only cop getting an award to-night.' His smile faded a little. 'Thank goodness.' He really didn't want to be the centre of attention.

She got that. 'You're the only one that matters to me.'

He glanced at his watch and breathed deep. 'Ready?'

So he was ignoring her compliment. 'As ready as I'll ever be.'

It had been an intense couple of hours as their flight from Queenstown had been delayed by weather for ninety minutes and then there'd been no taxis at the airport when they landed. Liam came to their rescue, picking them up and delivering them to the hotel with little time to get dressed. Maisie hugged him. 'Relax, gorgeous. Tonight's all about you.' His to enjoy and be celebrated for his bravery.

Her parents were also here. Liam had got them seats at their table because, as he'd said, they were as much Zac's parents as theirs. She knew he'd be ecstatic they'd come. Like they'd miss this occasion.

Zac took her hand and looked her up and down. 'You are so beautiful you make my heart sing.' He kissed her softly. 'Truly, you do.'

Her heart expanded with love. 'Don't make me cry or my mascara will run.'

And I'll be all choked up for hours.

'Let's do this.' As Zac's fingers slipped between hers, she sighed with happiness. Sometimes he worried her with his concerns about her getting hurt or her family not accepting their relationship but he was so wrong. Her life had become wonderful in such a short time it seemed unreal. It couldn't be any better, and she just wanted to take the lift to the rooftop and shout out across Christchurch, 'I'm in love with the most wonderful man on earth.'

Instead Zac pressed the button that'd take them down to the first floor. 'Showtime.' He grinned. 'I'm glad you're with me. I did not want to do this on my own.'

'You were never going to do that. The family's here, and so are your old mates from when you worked here.'

'Not the same,' he said, a little frown appearing.

'What's worrying you?'

And don't say, 'Nothing.'

'Nothing.' He bent to kiss her cheek. 'Promise.'

She didn't believe him, but the lift bumped to a halt and the doors slid open to reveal a well-dressed crowd of men and women standing around talking and laughing with glasses of champagne or beer in their hands. It was not time to have an argument over something that could just as easily turn out to be unimportant.

'About time.' Liam stepped away from a circle of people and came towards them.

Zac's hand tightened around hers like a reflex motion, and then he began to withdraw his hold.

Maisie tightened her grip. They were a couple, and she wasn't going to hide it. If the family hadn't got the idea already, then it was time they opened their eyes. But she believed they all knew she and Zac were an item. 'Hi, Liam. Where's Sasha?'

'Talking to her sister. The cop that introduced us, remember?' He wrapped an arm around Maisie in a hug. 'Good to see you here with Zac,' he said quietly. It was approval.

Letting Zac's hand go, she hugged her brother tight. 'Thanks.' Stepping away she felt the full force of Zac's eyes on them and knew he was expecting some kind of reaction from Liam. 'Zac's gone the whole distance with his attire tonight.' Her stomach was still doing its thing whenever she looked at him, he looked so gorgeous.

'You've scrubbed up all right.' Liam gave Zac a man hug. 'You ready for this?' There was understanding in her brother's eyes. He knew the memories would hit Zac when the speeches were made, but he also got it that Zac was moving on and tonight would help.

Zac grimaced, then looked from Liam to her and back, and stood a little taller. 'Yes, I am.'

'Good. Let's have a drink. I was about to give up waiting for you two to turn up.' Liam signalled a waitress, obviously taking command so that Zac could relax. It was how these two operated, their way of supporting each other.

'Champagne for me,' Maisie laughed. 'I'm celebrating tonight.'

'Zac, there you are.' Her mother pushed through the crowd to wrap her arms around him. 'You didn't think we'd miss this, did you?'

Zac blinked, then brushed his eyes with the back of a hand. 'Pippa, Ross, thank you for coming. You've made my night.'

Maisie grinned. 'You thought you couldn't get any more tickets for our table but Liam had already beaten you to it.' Zac had mentioned inviting them, and her mum had said they were going away for the weekend, fully intending to surprise him.

'Should've known.' Zac grinned. 'Families, eh?'

'You bet.' Her father shook his hand. 'We're yours.'

Zac blinked, turned away.

'Hi, Maisie, great to see you.' Sasha appeared beside her. 'What a stunning dress. That shade of blue suits you perfectly, and I'm a little jealous of how you can wear something so fitting and look perfect.'

Maisie blushed. 'Come on. You look wonderful too.'

Sasha laughed. 'Now we've got that out of the way, let's enjoy the night.' She was looking at Zac. 'Your man is looking exceptional tonight, isn't he?'

My man?

Yes, he was her man, and exceptional in more ways than one. 'I think so.'

A gong sounded. 'Would everyone go in and take their places at the tables now, thank you.'

'We *were* running close to the wire for getting here.' Zac took her elbow. What happened to holding her hand? Was he getting nervous? 'Ready for this?'

'Yes, I am.' She locked her eyes on him. 'So are you.'

His chest rose. 'You know what? I am. I can do anything with you by my side.'

I am not going to cry. I'm not. She wiped a tear away. *Okay, not much.*

'We're holding people up from getting to their tables.' They'd stopped in the middle of the main aisle running down the centre of the large room.

Zac grinned. 'Do I care?' Confident Zac to the fore. Completely to the fore. He talked and laughed with everyone around their table, accepted congratulations from strangers and friends alike, and all the time kept an eye out for her.

The evening flew by. The dinner courses came and went, her glass was constantly topped up by hovering waiters and the talk and laughter around their table was funny and enjoyable.

Then a man stepped onto the stage and tapped his glass. 'Can I have everyone's attention, please?'

'Here we go.' Liam tipped his head in Zac's direction.

'Ladies and gentlemen, let me introduce myself. I'm John Collins, Police District Commander.' Polite applause followed. Then, 'I'm not going to talk all night.'

A few good-natured comments came from around the room.

'But I am going to say that without all of

you our district wouldn't be as safe for the public as it is. Not that it's perfect by a long way, but I know from personal experience that all of you do your utmost for our people.'

'Get on with it,' Zac muttered.

Maisie reached for his hand, and he squeezed tight.

'Tonight we are recognising some exceptional members of the force.' Collins continued for a couple of minutes, then paused. 'Right, that's enough from me, except to say thank you to all of you, and especially to those receiving awards tonight. I'm now handing over to department director, Jeremy Harlen.'

'He's in charge of the station I worked at here in Christchurch,' Zac told her.

Harlen talked about the men and women to be honoured, then began calling each individual to the stage to get their pin and certificate. Maisie watched and listened, her heart pounding as it got closer to Zac's turn. It seemed to take for ever, then suddenly the wait was over.

'Detective Zachary Lowe, please come forward.'

Maisie squeezed his hand. 'Go you.'

'Want to come with me?'

'No, this is your show.'

His smile was crooked, but he nodded. 'True.'

By the time he reached the stage everyone was clapping. Maisie was crying. Damn it, she'd sworn she wouldn't do this. Impossible not to when Zac looked strong and confident, and so damned wonderful striding across to shake the commander's hand. She scrunched up the paper serviette her dad passed across to dab at her eyes.

Jeremy Harlen shook Zac's hand. So did John Collins before taking over the microphone. 'Now I am going to say a bit more than I've done so far. Most of you know the story of how one night fourteen months ago my team was called out to an armed holdup that went horribly wrong. Every man on our team worked hard to get a good outcome but we were on the back foot from the beginning. The men were armed and dangerous, and were not interested in reasoning their way out of the situation. One of ours lost his life.' John paused, swallowed hard. 'This man, Zac Lowe, took a bullet for me. I owe him my life.'

Collins wrapped Zac in a man hug as the room erupted with shouts of 'Bravo!' and 'Zac! Zac! Zac!'

Maisie gripped her hands together on her

lap and stared at Zac. He seemed to grow under the applause, like this was the last step in leaving the past behind.

The commander stepped forward and clasped Zac's hand, shook hard. 'We need men like you in our force.' He reached behind and picked up what looked like a medal and pinned it on Zac's jacket. 'For courage and bravery while serving our country.'

Again the room erupted with cheers and clapping. Zac raised a hand and gave a wave. 'Thank you, everyone. I appreciate this and the kind words, but I know others would've done the same if they'd been in the same position.' He shook hands with Collins and Harlen once more and walked off the stage.

'We won't see him for a while,' Liam laughed. 'Everyone will want a word with him.'

'Then let's get another round of drinks and have our own little party.' Sasha waved to a waitress. 'What do you think, Maisie?'

'Good idea.' Her glass was empty and she was in the mood to have some fun and let her hair down a little.

'Zac, got a minute?' Jeremy tilted his head towards a couple of empty chairs away from the tables.

Why did this feel like he was about to be put on the spot? Zac wondered as he said, 'Sure.' If he was being honest, he'd half expected Jeremy to want to have a chat. He was way overdue telling the chief his decision. He looked over to the table where Maisie sat with Liam and Sasha and his stomach knotted with love. He was doing the right thing, for them both. Maisie was the love of his life. Always had been, always would be.

'Want a beer?' Jeremy had the attention of a waiter.

'Make it a wine, thanks.' He wasn't driving anything more lethal than the lift up to his room tonight. And he was hyped. All the good-natured cheers and back-slapping had put him in high spirits. For the first time since the shooting he completely accepted what had happened and his role in it. He'd done his best and it had turned out to be good.

They parked their butts with their backs slightly to the room so that hopefully everyone got the idea and left them alone for a little while. Zac sipped his wine and waited for the inevitable.

'You're ready to come back,' Jeremy said. As an opener it was direct and blunt. Typical Jeremy.

He did miss the big cases, the long hours

that became nights and days as the team dug deeper into murders and drug dealers and all the other big crimes that went down in a city and which Queenstown was lucky not to experience very often. When he'd gone home to recover and make the decision about whether he wanted to continue his career in the CIB, he'd found he mostly preferred the quieter lifestyle of his hometown where there were people he knew and time to do more than work. Though there were days when he longed for the detecting work he'd been good at. Sometimes he thought he should return to doing that. But Maisie made his decision straightforward.

'I don't see you rushing to pack your bags,' Jeremy commented after a long moment of silence.

'I have a life down south.' It was true. In the space of fourteen months he'd established himself in S and R, had gained a reputation as a fair but hard cop, felt more at home than he had anywhere else. And again, there was Maisie. Whichever way he turned, everything came back to Maisie. She'd returned home to get back on her feet amongst those she loved. Queenstown was in her blood. She adored the mountains and space. None of those in Christchurch, no close friends or parents.

Even if he was busting to take up this offer, he couldn't ask her to move again. The job was tempting but not tempting enough to tip Maisie's life sideways again.

'You had one here.'

'All work and no play.' That's how he'd chosen to live back then. He'd never been concerned that he was alone because his career came first over everything. Strange how that all changed with one bullet. He'd gone back to his roots where people knew him as more than a detective. Back to where his career didn't run his life twenty-four-seven, and where he could be useful in other areas. He'd gone back to Queenstown because one day Maisie would come home. And she had.

'Bring her with you.' Jeremy inclined his head towards the table where Maisie sat.

So he'd noticed Maisie, and that they were together. Their changed relationship was no secret. Zac glanced over his shoulder to find her. She was watching him, a smile lightening her face. His gut squeezed. Bring Maisie to Christchurch when she'd only recently settled back in Queenstown where she always felt happiest? Where she could walk with her head high and not have to cope with the meanness of people who thought she was nearly as guilty as Paul. She'd have that here.

More so as no one knew her. Which wasn't a reason to drag her away from having Mallory and Kayla nearby. They shared so much, had a lot of background that couldn't be beaten by new friends in a new city. 'That isn't an option. For either of us.'

Jeremy waved a carrot in front of him. 'You'll have your own team.' Two carrots. 'An increase in salary. Plus me to talk over any problems arising with staff or cases.'

He couldn't want for more. Best job, best conditions. Crunch time. Get it over and done with. 'Thanks, but no thanks. I am happy where I am. I won't be returning to Christchurch to work.' Definite decision. His chest felt light and free. When he'd left after the shooting, it had been with the knowledge there was a position back here when he was ready. At first he'd thought he'd only be away a few months but he'd barely thought about it since, that's how right it felt to be in Queenstown. Zac stood up and shook Jeremy's hand. 'I appreciate your offer, but it wouldn't work out for me.'

On the way back to his woman, he picked up two glasses of champagne off a waiter's tray. Handing her one, he tapped it with his. 'To us.'

'And to Zac for what tonight means,' said

Liam. The family, his family, were all raising their glasses in his direction. Maisie was
beaming. His heart stuttered when he met
Ross's eye. It said, 'Be careful with Maisie.'

I'm doing my best.

Was it enough?

'So how's my hero?' Maisie snuggled into
Zac as the lift shot them up to the eleventh
floor. It had been quite the night and she was
buzzing, more than ready for some hot activ-
ity with Zac.

'Wired.' He grinned and pulled her close,
his mouth covering hers.

'Perfect.' She pressed closer, her breasts
hard against his chest, her mouth opening
under his. Felt his need pressing into her
belly. Felt her own grow, spreading heat over
her body. Her legs trembled; her skin tightened.

Zac lifted his head far enough to murmur,
'Maisie, Maisie,' then went back to kissing
her senseless.

She was floating on air. This kiss beat the
heck out of others they'd shared. She was with
Zac, in a hotel, and about to make love. Love.
As in hearts joined for ever. Not that Zac ever
mentioned love, but he showed her in a mil-
lion little ways—his smile, bringing a coffee

over from his apartment when he got up to go to work if they hadn't spent the night together, his sensational, toe-curling kisses. So tonight she was celebrating *them*.

'Um…excuse us.'

Maisie jerked back, looked around. The lift was open, people were standing outside waiting to come in. Had they gone up to their level and returned without noticing? Or hadn't they left the conference room floor?

'Ah, sorry about that.' Zac reached for her, pressed her head against his chest. 'Do you want to share the lift?' His chest and stomach were making small convulsions like he was silently laughing.

She couldn't help it. She began laughing too. What the heck? Might as well make a complete idiot herself. Slipping her hand into Zac's, she leaned back against the wall and tapped her foot as the lift filled and began to move upwards, stopping at every damned floor on the way to theirs. She couldn't even blame anyone for the delay. She and Zac had lost all awareness of where they were, only wanting to be close together.

Being dragged back to reality made her smile. She'd make time to change out of her dress before they got too hot and busy. She'd gone shopping yesterday for some fancy lingerie that cost a bundle and was worth every cent. Even if she said so, she looked sexy in the red satin and lace shorts and top with thin straps that showed her cleavage to perfection.

She headed for her case before he had the door to their room closed. 'Give me five.'

'Five? I can't wait thirty seconds.' He reached for her.

'Tough.' Ducking out of the way, she snatched up the lingerie and stepped into the bathroom. 'You're going to have to.' Emotion clogged her throat as she tugged her dress over her head and tossed it aside. Reaching for the lingerie she rubbed the soft satin against her feverish skin. Cool and sensual. The strawberry shade highlighted her blond hair as she gave it a quick brush. Then she applied a new shade of lipstick to match and she was ready to go.

Pausing, she stared at herself in the mirror. This was it. A commitment to the man she truly loved. Zac was her man.

The thin heels of her shoes clicked on the tiles as she left the bathroom. Holding her head high, and her shoulders up, she crossed to the bedroom room and right up to him.

Zac's heart leapt in his chest. 'Maisie, sweetheart, you're so beautiful you take my breath away.' Literally. He was struggling to get any air into his lungs. Placing his hands on her hips, he held her back far enough to gaze down that red-covered length, over the curves of her breasts, the flat stomach and beyond.

She was stretching up into the points of those incredible shoes, her mouth seeking his. Her sweet mouth, now hot and fierce, as though she was claiming him. Which she was. He was hers for her to do with as she wanted. Starting with this kiss.

Soft. Gentle. Demanding. Sexy. Everything he'd ever hoped for—and more. Lots more. Holding her body up against his, his mouth covering, taking, hers, his hands spread across her back, he began walking slowly backwards to the massive bed where chocolates lay on the pillows and seductive lights highlighted the beauty he held. Absorbing her heat and softness, tasting her sweetness and fire, he put one foot back, then the other, taking her with him as he kissed her. A deep, hot, for ever kiss. A kiss to seal their relationship. 'Maisie, you are so beautiful.'

Her mouth spread into a wide smile under his lips. He thought she whispered 'Zac' into his mouth, or he could've been dreaming because everything was like a dream right now, only so much better, hotter, softer, more loving. Real.

Cooler air slid across his lower back. Maisie's hands were splayed across his heated skin, tightening his abs, centring his being, hardening his need. 'Slow down, woman.' He couldn't lose control. Maisie came first. He swung her up into his arms, and strode the last few metres to lay her on the bed, before shucking off his clothes as fast as possible.

She reached up, pulled him so he sprawled across her, feeling her breasts pressing against his chest, those slim legs under his thighs. And still she kissed him, teased him. 'Zac,' she whispered against his skin. 'I want you.' She was pushing up onto an elbow to lean over and lick his nipples, flaming the fire in his belly.

Reaching for her, he rolled over, tucked her under him and began to slowly return the compliment, licking, kissing, devouring her body. Stopping there to touch that pale soft skin, moving to kiss a trail down from her neck to her breasts and on down the cleft between them to her belly button. Kissing all the way as she arched up beneath him, pushing against him, crying out with longing filling her voice, touching his erection. Stirring him harder. Had him caressing those thighs that had often made him long to touch her. Smooth, hot.

'Please, Zac,' she begged. 'Take me, now. I can't wait.'

Nor could he. But he would. Finding her centre, touching her, feeling her moist heat, nearly undid him. And when she quivered against his hand he rose over her and slid inside his Maisie. Pulling back, he gasped for air, and drove into her again. And again until she cried out, and then he let go and joined her. He'd found what he'd been searching for. Maisie and love all in one.

CHAPTER ELEVEN

MAISIE AWOKE SLOWLY, stretching her legs to the end of the bed and her arms over her head. There were aches in places she didn't know existed. Good aches. Rolling her head, she blinked. 'Zac?' Where was he? The bathroom door was open.

'Hey.' A quiet word from by the window where he sat. The curtain was drawn back enough for him to look out.

Shuffling her backside up the bed, she leaned against the headboard. 'You been awake long?'

'About an hour.' His voice was flat. After last night and making love twice?

Something wasn't right. 'What's up?'

'It was a big night. I think it's all catching up with me.' He didn't give her a blinding smile to say it had been fantastic.

She wasn't about to let him spoil the day,

or the night before. 'What time are we meeting the others for brunch?'

'In an hour. I was about to shake you awake.'

'Kissing me awake would work better.' She smiled.

'Then we might not make it to brunch.'

So they were still okay. He was just worn out. And she'd been thinking of herself, not him. Climbing out of bed, she crossed to wrap her arms around him from behind. 'You're amazing. I haven't had such a wonderful time in for ever.'

Turning, he looked up at her. 'Nor have I.'

Leaning down she kissed his cheek, then his mouth. 'I think we're past the dating phase, don't you?'

Zac stood up, pulled her in close. 'Well and truly.' He kissed her, long and deep.

All was good. 'I'd better grab a shower.'

He took her hand and headed for the bathroom. 'We're going to be late.'

A while later, as they were dressing, Maisie asked, 'What did Jeremy Harlen want last night? You two were in a huddle for quite a while.'

Zac winced. 'He offered me my old job back. I knew it was likely to happen, been expecting it for months.'

'Zac?' Alarm bells were ringing. He'd never mentioned this before, though when he first returned to Queenstown he had said something about how long he might stay in town. She'd forgotten all about that. 'You accepted it?'

He shook his head abruptly, concentrated too much on doing up his shirt buttons. 'No, I turned it down.'

'Why?'

Zac shrugged. 'I'm happy where I am.'

Deep breath. 'Are you sure?'

He came to her then and took her face in his hands, his eyes locking with hers. 'Yes, absolutely.'

So kiss me.

He didn't.

'That's good, but I know how much you loved that job.' The quaver in her voice was a dead giveaway. She was fearful for what lay ahead, that he might change his mind despite his insistence he wouldn't. He had loved working up here. An ache was starting up in her heart. She trusted Zac not to hurt her.

'I did, but it's over. I live and work in Queenstown now.' His hands fell away but he was still watching her.

Doubts slammed in left and right. Was she the woman he wanted? Had he had a sudden change of heart and she was no longer important enough to be with? Did he really want to leave her to come back here and was putting off telling her? Had Zac already reached the point where he didn't think she was enough for him?

Slow down. You're going off the deep end without reason.

Fear of being hurt again wasn't reason? Fear of having her trust thrown in her face didn't count? She drew a steadying breath, huffed it out. 'This isn't anything to do with us, is it?'

'Maisie, I don't want to leave you, not for anything. And I couldn't expect you to pack up and move again when you've only just returned home.'

'Is that why you turned the position down? Because of me?' And she'd thought they should talk about everything.

'*One* of the reasons. Not the main one.'

Forget the main one. 'You made a decision involving both of us without talking to me first? My opinion doesn't count?'

'You don't know anyone in Christchurch.' Desperation filled his eyes. 'I was thinking of you.'

'Over-protecting me again, that's what you're doing.' She glared at him. 'Will you never accept I'm all grown up and quite capable of making and living with my own choices?'

'I don't want you unhappy, Mais.'

'What do you think you're saving me from? A challenge? Fun and excitement at starting something new with you? This isn't how close, loving relationships work, Zac. We're meant to work together on everything—talk about the big issues, come to conclusions together.' Sinking onto the side of the bed, she stared at the floor. 'I didn't even know you might've wanted to come back here.'

She'd given one hundred percent of herself to Zac—like she had to Paul. Too much? Or had she made another monumental mistake? Trusted Zac to believe in her too easily?

'I tossed the idea around a bit at first, but wasn't rushing to grab the opportunity. Then when you came home, I more or less forgot about it. You're what's important to me, Maisie. You and me as a couple.'

'We're not a couple when you don't discuss important issues with me, and a job offer is right up there.' She couldn't believe he'd hurt her. She'd trusted him not to. 'I have to know what's going on or I feel like I'm not in a partnership.' Which was just how Paul had treated her—someone supposed to follow, not stand beside him. She could not go with that again. Not even with Zac, whom she trusted.

Silence fell between them.

Except for the crashing under her ribs.

Say something, Zac.

Nothing.

She stood up. 'We'd better get a move on. The others will be wondering what's happened to us.'

'Maisie,' Zac whispered. 'I'm sorry.'

'It would be better if you just talked to me.'

He took her face in his gentle hands and leaned in to kiss her. Slowly, tentatively, as if he hadn't done this before.

She stepped back. If he wasn't going let her into his life fully, then they didn't really have a relationship—not one she could live with.

Zac's head was thumping. He'd made the biggest mistake of his life and didn't know how to rectify it. Maisie was hurt. He'd broken her trust in him by making decisions involving her without her input. He wasn't good at loving her.

Head high, she strode into the café ahead of him, having remained silent on the short walk from the hotel. He'd never known her to cut him off like this before. The disappointment directed at him when she learned why he'd turned down the job would stay with him for a long time.

Hard to believe they'd made love twice during the night. He hadn't been able resist her the first time when she came out of the bathroom in that sexy-as-could-be red lingerie and they'd fallen together, everything coming together so fast. Then when she was curled into his body and holding him like he was the most important person in her life, he'd had to have her again, and he'd made love extra gently and drawn out her orgasm until she was begging him for release.

He'd been so relaxed and happy. But as the hours crept by with Maisie tucked in against him, he'd thought about the conversation he'd had with Jeremy. How he'd be able to run his own department, something he'd been aiming for before the shooting. Then he'd thought about his job in Queenstown and how much he enjoyed being back home. Especially now that he and Maisie were getting along like a house on fire. *Had been* getting along. Because right now there was nothing but ice in her eyes, in her tense shoulders and white-knuckled fingers gripping her bag.

'Morning-after blues got you?' Liam asked quietly.

'Something like that,' he admitted. 'It was quite a night.' In more ways than one.

'Maisie's very quiet too.' Brother to the fore.

As if Zac needed reminding that Liam would cut him out if he hurt his sister. Something else to worry about. 'She didn't sleep very well.' They'd been busy.

'Look after her, Zac.' The warning was there, loaded and ready to explode into him.

'Of course.' He had been when he told Jeremy no thanks. *Stop protecting me.* Maisie had a point. He had tried to back off on that lately but it was hard to give up what he'd been doing since he was seventeen. He was between a rock and a hard place. He hadn't used her as the only reason not to return here. He genuinely liked his job in Queenstown, the different pace suited him now. And yes, there were things he'd regret about not taking up the position he'd been offered last night, but they weren't the most important facts. That was living where Maisie was, and say what she liked, leaving home when she'd just arrived back wouldn't be easy for her. Queenstown was home to both of them, and he wanted their family nearby if they set up house together and got married. Also if they had kids. Except right now that was looking impossible.

The eggs were glue in his mouth. Coffee

didn't wash them down. His stomach was rotating, his head thumping.

Maisie was pushing a hash brown around her plate, looking at it as though it might bite.

'Not hungry?' Ross asked from across the table.

'Not really,' he admitted.

Maisie didn't answer.

He stood abruptly. 'I'll go and check us out of the hotel.' There hadn't been time to do it when they left and he couldn't sit still another moment.

'I'll come with you.' Maisie put down her knife and fork, drained her coffee and got up to hug her brother. 'See you for Mum and Dad's anniversary.'

'I can drop you at the airport,' Liam replied, one eye on his sister and one on him.

Maisie shook her head. 'Thanks, but we've got plenty of time and you need to go with Sasha to see her family.'

Liam nodded. 'True,' He looked in two minds about leaving his sister with Zac.

Zac stepped up. 'Maisie and I'll be fine. Plenty of taxis on the rank last time I looked.'

Sasha was hugging Maisie and they were talking quietly.

'Zac? What's going on? You two had a lover's tiff?'

'Nothing like that, mate.'

'Whatever's putting that look on your faces, fix it. It doesn't suit either of you.' Liam turned away to take Sasha's hand, looked back at him. 'See you both when we come down for the anniversary shindig.'

'Will do.' If he was still welcome when the family learned why he and Maisie weren't talking at the moment. In three weeks Liam and Maisie's parents would be celebrating forty years married. Forty years of happiness and love, with life's problems thrown in which they'd managed to work their way through and remain loyal and in love.

Maisie hugged her mum and dad. 'See you when you get back on Friday.' They were taking a short road trip on the way south.

Ross looked over to him, said, 'It was a good night.' Then he looked at his daughter and back to him. 'Keep it that way.'

That sharp tone took him back to his teenage years and Ross warning him to stay clear of Maisie. But no one appeared to mind them being together now—unless he screwed up big time. Then who knew? 'Of course.' He'd do his best anyhow. Problem being Maisie had a mind of her own and he'd hurt her by not involving her in his decision. It wasn't going to be easy to get past this blunder, given her past with Paul.

She walked beside him out of the café, head high again, shoulders tight, and gripping her handbag as though someone was about to steal it.

He strode along, slowed when he realised he was walking too fast and making her have to take longer steps than were comfortable. 'Sorry,' he muttered.

'Where did I go wrong?'

Gulp. 'You didn't. Haven't.'

'You've made a choice and it isn't what I thought we were doing together.'

'I did.'

'Should be an exciting flight home.'

An hour later they sat awkwardly on hard plastic row chairs in a corner of the departure lounge at Christchurch Airport, cardboard mugs of unwanted coffee on the seats either side of them. Zac's legs stretched ahead of him as he stared at his shoes, wondering how he'd got into this position. He loved Maisie. Everything had been going well between them. It should be simple to tell her he loved her and drop everything else. If only he knew how to say 'I love you' without worrying that he wasn't loveable. He'd been eight when he'd told his mother he loved her and she'd walked away without a smile, nor had she said a word. The pain had been deep and lasting. 'I want so much for this to work out between us.'

The colour left her cheeks. 'What are you saying?'

He tried, and failed, to ignore the sorrow in her eyes. 'This has shown me I'm not the man you deserve,' he growled through the tears stuck in the back of his throat.

She didn't even blink.

He didn't know what he'd expected, but nothing wasn't it. 'You're not surprised, judging by your reaction.'

'Surprised?' Now she blinked. 'Surprised?' she almost shouted. 'Try disappointed. Hurt. I trusted you, Zac.'

Slam. His heart stalled. Trusted. In the past. 'Where does this leave us? Our friendship? The family?' Her questions were so quiet he had to lean in to hear her, and was rewarded with the familiar scent he'd come to adore. It teased him, reminding him of what was at stake. 'Don't say we can have a conversation and get on with where we left off. It's not that easy. I've been there before, had the conversations with Paul, heard how he hadn't done anything wrong and that I had to believe in him, and look where that left me. I said I'd never go there again, Zac, and this mightn't seem like a big deal to you, but it reeks of being let down badly to me.'

'Maisie, you came home to get your mojo back.' *Try harder, man.* 'You're happy in Queenstown with Mallory and Kayla settled there, your parents only a few minutes away. Then we get together.' He still hadn't told her his true feelings, but if he did now she'd probably see it as an attempt to win her back. Which it would be. He opened his mouth, saw Liam and Ross in his mind and closed it again. Don't hurt her any more.

'They are my closest friends, not my reason for getting up in the morning.' Her hands were making folds in the hem of her shirt. Her face was white, and her eyes dull with sadness when her gaze locked on him. 'You're not being entirely honest with me, Zac, and that's the cruellest part. It's the first time that I know of when you haven't told me what you're really feeling. That is hard to take or understand.' Her breasts rose as she drew a breath. 'Are you being honest with yourself?'

He winced.

'Your silence speaks volumes. It says you don't really love me enough to continue our relationship. I thought you'd have the guts to tell me, but I wonder if I've ever really known you as well as I believed. Which is awful because I relied on my impression of you as honest and reliable, and caring and loving. I believed you were the man I loved and wanted to spend the rest of my life with.' She stood up and reached for her carry-on bag. 'I thought I could trust you. I guess I was wrong.'

'I don't bloody believe it,' Maisie cried into her sodden pillow three nights later. 'When I fall for Zac, the most trustful man I know, he goes and leaves me hanging.' She couldn't accept that he mightn't talk about the important things they'd face if they shared a life together. He often held worries close to his chest, but they didn't involve her. Or so she'd thought.

She loved him. That hadn't changed. It wouldn't go away overnight. It wouldn't go away at all. She'd never told him in those exact words, but surely he'd seen how much she did love him. He'd never mentioned the L word either, yet most of the time she'd believed he did love her.

It just went to show she couldn't trust a man with her heart again. If Zac could do this, then what chance was there of her ever getting it right? None. Nada. Zero.

Her heart hadn't stopped aching since Sunday morning. It ached when she was nursing her little patients, when she shopped for groceries she then didn't eat, and all night long it kept her awake. She'd lost the man she'd come to love as much as life because it turned out Zac was afraid to take a chance on her loving him enough so he could be open about what he wanted to do with his career and, therefore, their future. He'd also obviously forgotten she needed to be in the picture all the time if they were going to have a stable relationship. But in the end, she loved Zac and someone had to make a move to sort this out. She could be the one to do that by knocking on Zac's door and suggesting they keep trying to make it work out. Yet she was reluctant. If he didn't trust her, she could be losing a future that would mean Zac and children. A family of her own to cherish all her life. She doubted she'd have that with anyone now because she'd always be waiting for the axe to fall.

Her phone beeped as a text came in.

She ignored it.

As she had Mallory and Kayla for days now. Fobbing them off with fibs about work and double shifts, because she felt such an idiot for even believing she could trust Zac.

She wasn't going to get away with it for much longer though. They also knew her too well.

Next she'd have to face her parents and pretend to be happy and all was good in her world. Might have to visit a make-up artist first and get painted up so the worry wasn't showing so much.

Why don't you like talking to me about us, Zac? You talked about the shooting and your fear and shock. Surely that was far more difficult than asking me if I'd move to Christchurch with you? That hurts as much as anything. Aren't I good enough for you?

She stared at the ceiling. No answers up there.

Tossing the covers aside, she crawled out of bed and groaned. She was so damned tired every muscle ached, her head throbbed and her heart was heavy. Might be time to join a gym or take up running to expend some energy and make sleeping a natural part of her routine again. Except she didn't have any energy, which had to be the reason sleep had evaded her since Zac did his number on her.

Pulling a jersey over her PJ top and picking up her phone, she trudged into the kitchen to make coffee. Her phone began blinking. More texts.

Grr... Leave me alone.

Another one from Kayla. She'd better deal with her friends. *Tap, tap*.

Need a catch-up. Things to talk about.

Time to tell them she and Zac were over. She'd held out on the misguided belief that Zac would come knocking on her door to promise he'd never make that mistake again, but he was probably waiting for her to go over and forgive him. She could do that, but she'd always be afraid of him doing it again. Her heart was broken and she needed to talk to someone.

The doorbell buzzed. Wouldn't be Zac. He'd just come straight on up. Might not with the way things were though.

The ringing didn't stop, was a continuous high-pitched noise slicing into her head. 'Coming.'

The ringing still didn't stop.

Unlocking the door, she pulled it open to find the young girl from next door staring up at her, tears running down her face.

Bending down, she said, 'Matilda? What's the matter?'

'Mummy's hurt. She's not talking.'

Slamming the door shut behind her, she took Matilda's hand. 'Come on, we'll go and see what's the matter.' Anna was hurt, not talking. It didn't sound good, if Matilda had got it right. The girl looked terrified. Reaching down she lifted her into her arms as she strode to her neighbour's front door. 'Is Daddy at home?'

'No. He went to work.'

She charged up the stairs. 'Anna? Can you hear me?'

'She won't talk to me,' Matilda said.

'Where is she?'

'In the kitchen.'

Anna lay sprawled across the floor, eyes closed, blood gushing from a head wound, and her right arm tucked under her back.

Maisie put Matilda down on a chair at the table. 'Stay there, sweetheart, while I ring for help and look after Mummy, okay?'

Matilda nodded slowly.

Kneeling down beside Anna, Maisie noted a yellowish puddle on the floor. Cooking oil, by the look of it. Anna must've skidded in it. 'Anna? It's Maisie.'

No movement, no recognition of her voice.

Maisie still had her phone in her hand. Quickly she punched a number. 'Zac, I'm at Anna and Mathew's. Get over here fast.' Click. She pressed one-one-one and holding the phone to her ear began feeling for Anna's pulse. Multi-tasking came easily to her.

'Emergency services. Which service do you require?'

'Ambulance.' Pulse steady.

'What's up?' Zac blasted into the room. 'Oh, crikey. Hey, Matilda, come here, little one.' He scooped her up into his arms and held her so she couldn't see her mother, all the while looking at Anna. 'Want me to take the phone? I'm presuming you're on to the ambulance?'

'Yes.' Giving him the phone, she added, 'Tell them Anna's unconscious, has a head wound. Looks like she slipped and hit the edge of the bench.' There was a red smear on the rim of the bench.

Lifting Anna's eyelids, she saw her eyes were dilated. Breathing slow but not dangerous. Heart rate rapid. One wound on the skull. Left arm uninjured. Right arm twisted badly at the shoulder. She'd leave that until the paramedics arrived. No abdominal swelling. Legs were straight. 'Head and shoulder, arm injury,' she told Zac.

He was giving the service Anna's address. 'There's a nurse with her.' He mentioned the injuries. 'You want me to stay on the line? Fine.'

Maisie got up to get the roll of paper towels from the bench. 'These will have to do for a wad until the ambulance gets here. I hope Kayla's on.' She was a first-rate advanced paramedic who never got fazed in urgent situations.

'You know where Mathew is?'

'Matilda said he went to work.'

'I don't have his number.'

'It's on the fridge door,' Matilda piped up. 'And Mummy's. There, under the princess.'

Maisie smiled as she reached for the notepaper with two phone numbers written clearly on it. Handing it to Zac, she rubbed her hand over Matilda's arm. 'You're a very brave girl. You did the right thing coming to get me.'

On the floor Anna began gasping and shaking.

Convulsions. Just what she didn't need, but not uncommon after head injury. Maisie held her head to the side and, using her finger, scooped Anna's tongue straight so she didn't choke. Even then she didn't relax, kept watching until Anna stopped convulsing.

'Hello, this is Zac Lowe, from the police station. I need to speak to Mathew, please.' He had his phone against his ear now.

Maisie held Anna's head until she settled completely.

'Get him out of the meeting. This is an emergency.' Then, 'Thank you.' He did an elaborate eye roll. 'Honestly.'

Picking up the roll of towels, Maisie tore off the first two and put them aside, then made a wad from the uncontaminated ones. 'Careful of little ears when talking to Dad.' Telling a policeman what to say? *Good one, Maisie.* She glanced at him.

He was smiling at her ever so cautiously.

There was a turn around. Any smile at all had to be better than none. She got on with stemming the blood flow from Anna's head.

'Mathew, Zac. Anna's had a fall. You need to come home.' Pause. 'Good man. See you shortly.' Another pause. 'Yes, she's fine. She's the hero in this. Tell you when you get here.' He hung up and slipped his phone in his pocket. 'On his way.'

A siren was coming closer by the second. 'Thank goodness,' Maisie muttered. 'We need them now.'

He shut off Maisie's phone. 'I'll go down to show them the way.' He still held Matilda close.

Hopefully the trauma of seeing an ambulance would be far less than watching her mother lying on the floor, though from the moment Zac had picked her up, Matilda hadn't been able to see Anna.

Heavy footsteps told her she had company. 'Thank goodness it's you,' she told Kayla as her friend stepped into the kitchen. 'Watch out. There's oil on the floor I haven't had time to clean up.'

'Will do.' Kayla was already sussing out their patient. 'Fill me in.'

It didn't take long, the details being scant. 'Not sure about that shoulder. Could be the upper arm that's damaged. Thought it best to wait until we roll her onto the stretcher. Especially with that head wound.' She wasn't sure how severe it was and didn't want to make matters worse.

'I agree.' Kayla was making her own observations while the other ambulance officer was attaching monitor pads to Anna's chest to take readings of heart rate, pulse and temperature.

Fast and efficient, they soon had Anna ready to roll onto her side so Maisie and Kayla could carefully move her arm to the side.

'Fractured wrist. Possible fracture to the humerus, definitely severe bruising to the upper arm muscles,' Kayla noted. 'Head wound's the major concern. Right, let's get her on the stretcher and we'll be on our way.'

When they were ready to go downstairs, Zac handed Matilda to Maisie. 'Here you go, my girl. Maisie will look after you while I help Mummy.' Two female ambulance crew and he wasn't standing back while they did the heavy lifting.

Kneeling down to tackle the oil spillage, Maisie's heart turned over. Typical. He was a man's man, stepping up to help, and all the better for it. Damn, but she'd missed him these few days. It had been especially hard when she only had to look out the window to see him in his kitchen or on his deck whenever he was at home. She was being stubborn by staying away. All because she had trust issues that had nothing to do with Zac. He'd never deliberately hurt her, and if he did get it wrong like last week, then she needed to let go the past and talk to him openly and honestly.

The sound of brakes skidding on the drive cut through everything. Mathew called out, 'What's happened? Anna? Oh, hell, what's wrong with her?'

'Daddy?'

Maisie raced downstairs, Matilda bouncing on her hip. 'Mathew, over here.'

He rushed to grab his daughter out of her arms and hug Matilda tight. His face was white as he stared over Matilda's head to the back of the ambulance. 'Maisie? Tell me what happened.'

'I think Anna slipped on some cooking oil. There was a puddle on the kitchen floor. She's hit her head as she fell.'

'Is she all right?'

Deep breath. 'Mathew, she's unconscious. I can't say more than that.' Life could change in a second. A person could lose everything without any warning. Where was Zac?

'What aren't you telling me?'

Zac came up just then. 'What Maisie's saying is she's not a doctor. She's done everything possible for Anna while waiting for the ambulance, and the paramedics have been brilliant too. Now it's important to get her to hospital so the doctors can take over.' As he spoke the ambulance began backing down the drive.

Again Maisie's heart softened. Zac was her man. He just didn't get it—yet. No, he did. It was her who had to let go the past completely and show him how much she loved him. Starting now. Would he let her in again? Or say she'd made his mistake into something too big to be able to forget in a hurry?

'And, Mathew,' Zac continued. 'Your daughter saved Anna. She ran to Maisie for help.'

Tears appeared in the corners of Mathew's eyes as he hugged his girl tighter.

Maisie gave him a moment, then said, 'Do you want a lift to the hospital?'

It took him a moment to gather himself. 'Thanks, but I'll drive us there. I'll just take a few minutes to calm down.'

'You're sure? I'd hate you to have an accident.'

'I'll take you.' Zac was on the same page.

'All right. Thanks. I'll get Matilda's car seat.' Mathew's voice was quavering, and his hands shaking.

'Wise move. I'll lock up after you've gone,' Maisie told him. Then she could go and get out of her PJ's and into a hot shower. This hadn't been the ideal start to her day.

Life could be damned short, Zac growled. No one knew when they got up in the morning what was going to happen during the day. According to Kayla when the paramedics took her into the emergency department, Anna was seriously ill. She might've slipped or she might've had a stroke. It would be a while before they knew, and Mathew was going to have to sit it out, poor man. Thankfully, he had family in town who were on their way to be with him. But what a shock to have to face.

Zac pulled into his drive. So why was he stuffing around waiting for Maisie to forgive him and not beating down her door to tell her he loved her more than anyone or anything? Why was he messing with something so beautiful? The love he'd longed for all his life had been in the palm of his hand and then he'd gone and blown it. She'd walked away because he'd acted like her ex.

He could blame his parents for not having love in his life when he was younger, but the fact remained he had been loved by others all his adult life and he'd been a coward to run from Maisie's hurt. He'd had support from a different quarter all his life, and it had seen him through everything. He loved Maisie. He loved her family, but they came second to what he felt for her. He should've known that from the start and acted accordingly. They wouldn't turn him away for loving their daughter and sister. They'd embrace him. And if he made mistakes—who didn't?—they'd be there to guide him as they had done with every damned thing throughout his life since the day he met them.

He had to persuade Maisie to give him another chance.

He'd hurt her big time. Yet she hadn't turned her back on him, not completely. He was the person she phoned first this morning to help with Anna. Admittedly, he lived next door, but a nurse lived over the road too. He was her go-to man, and he was going to remain as such for the rest of their lives.

Shoving the car door wide, he got out and straightened his shoulders. Here goes. He'd be honest and upfront. Maisie would understand that better than any other approach. He desperately needed her to understand and forgive him.

Her front door was locked. He pressed the bell continuously. Nothing. Probably in the shower washing the sleep out of her face and eyes. Dealing with Anna, still in her pyjamas with her hair coming out of the band she must've put it in before going to bed, she'd looked exhausted. His heart had cracked a little when he saw her talking on the phone to the emergency line. Hard to believe he'd managed to stay away for three whole days and nights.

And now she wasn't answering her doorbell. He couldn't blame her for avoiding him if that's what she was doing.

He crossed to his apartment and let himself in. Not locked, because he'd forgotten all about that when he drove Mathew and his daughter to the hospital. Tossing the car keys on the sideboard, he took the stairs two at a time, and tripped to a stop on the top one. Maisie sat slumped on a stool, a steaming mug in her hands. His black bathrobe was far too large on her slim frame. Her wet hair hung in a long twist down her back. Most of all, she looked shattered.

'Maisie, are you all right?'

'I locked myself out,' she muttered. 'Helped myself to your shower.'

Thank goodness for that. He strode across and took the mug out of her hands before wrapping her in his arms. 'Darling, I'm so damned sorry for being an idiot.'

Her head was moving from side to side. 'You've been saying that since you were a teen. But it's me who's the idiot this time.'

'No, you were looking out for yourself.' He drew a rough breath. 'I don't usually call you darling.'

Careful, you're not out of the mess by a long shot.

Using one hand, he pulled up another stool and sat down, still holding her.

'Don't try to charm me over, Zac. It isn't going to work.' Her eyes were dark but there was a glimmer of a spark in them.

'I was speaking from my heart.' It was true. He wasn't going to hold anything back any

more. 'I made a hideous mistake and I want
to rectify it. If I can.'

'Zac, I was wrong to get so steamed up
and walk away from you. It felt so like what's
happened in the past I didn't stop to think
about the fact that this is you, and you don't
deliberately try to hurt people, especially me.
It's my turn to say sorry.'

'I love you.' The words flew out, as they
should, full of love, of emotion, of everything
he had to give. Far easier to say than he'd ever
have believed. 'Maisie.' He gripped her shaking hands. 'I do. I love you and have right
from when we first met.'

Her head bobbed down once, then she
locked a fierce look on him. 'I love you too,
Zac. I think I probably always have too. That
day at school when you walked away from me
I wanted you to stay, not as a kind of brother,
but as my boyfriend.'

The tension left him. 'I had to go or risk
getting kicked out of your family, which
frightened the hell out of me. I'd finally found
the kind of love I'd been looking for since I
was born. Your parents gave me that without question. I wasn't losing it, even for you
then. We were young and there was no future for us back then. We had some growing

up to do. But now's different. I'm ready for everything.'

'I panicked on Sunday. I'd had moments worrying about would happen if our relationship failed. Then you told me about why you'd turned down the job and everything came crashing in on top of me. I didn't mean to hurt you.'

'I did say I wanted to remain in Queenstown, that asking you to move away from here wasn't the only reason I said no to the position.'

'I ignored that.'

'You did, but that's okay. I've forgotten already.'

Maisie started to say something.

He cut her off. 'We are so close, so into each other, each other's other half, really. I only ever wanted you, and yet I wasn't one hundred percent ready to let go my fears about screwing up with you and therefore losing everyone. But after seeing Anna lying on the floor, I realise life's too short to waste on arguments and worrying about what might or might not happen. I want us to be together, facing life side by side, Maisie.'

'You need to learn to trust me, us.'

'I do now. Though I might need a nudge occasionally.'

She pulled her hands free and picked up her mug to take a sip. 'Paul broke my trust. I never believed you'd do that.'

'Yet I did.' His heart died a little bit. She wasn't going to forgive him.

'Yes, you did. You made me believe I'll never be able to trust my heart to any man again.'

He was in deep trouble. 'Maisie, I am so sorry. I do love you, and I won't ever let you down like that again.'

The mug turned back and forth in her hands. 'The thing is, at first I wondered if I was falling for you because I could trust you not to hurt me.' She looked away for a moment and when her gaze returned her eyes were sad and sorry.

He sucked in a sharp breath.

'But it didn't take long for me to know I love you for the man you are, all of you, all your quirky personality streaks and the honest ones, serious and not so smart ones.'

His lungs squeezed the air back out.

Her eyes softened, as did her face, and those gorgeous lips, her whole stance following. 'Zac, I have been dying to say this for weeks. I love you with all my heart. I've come home to you, with you, for you.'

Relief soared through him, set his heart beating wildly. Maisie loved him.

She hadn't finished, but that was his Maisie. 'We've both made mistakes. Let's not do that again. As friends we've always been able to talk. Let's keep doing that as lovers.'

He scooped her up in his arms and lowered his mouth to hers. 'Sweetheart, thank you. I love you so much it hurts.' His world was falling into place at last.

Except for one more thing. He pulled out of her arms, and dropped to his knee. 'Maisie Rogers, please marry me and have a family with me.'

She laughed. And cried. And ran her hands down both sides of his face. 'Get up. We're equals, remember.'

'You're killing me,' he said, scrambling onto his feet.

She stood up, breasts to his chest, and smiled through her tears. 'Of course I'll marry you and have some babies with you. Bring it all on.'

Then they were kissing like there was no tomorrow; only there would be. Plenty if Zac got his way.

An hour later Maisie picked up her phone from where she'd left it when Zac turned up.

Two identical texts from Mallory and Kayla:

What are we going to talk about?

Maisie laughed.

Wedding plans.

* * * * *

If you missed the previous story in the Queenstown Search & Rescue trilogy, then check out

A Single Dad to Rescue Her

If you enjoyed this story, discover these other great reads from Sue MacKay

**Captivated by Her Runaway Doc
The GP's Secret Baby Wish
The Nurse's Secret**

All available now!